The Hartpury Horror

J.D. Warner

The Hartpury Horror

THE
UNSEEING
EYE

TALLINN, 2020

This is a work of fiction. Names, characters, businesses, places, events, locales, and incidents are either the products of the author's imagination or used in a fictitious manner. Any resemblance to actual persons, living or dead, or actual events is purely coincidental.

First paperback edition,
Published in 2020 by The Unseeing Eye
in Tallinn, Estonia

Cover concept by Attila Orosz
Cover image of Hugo Jenkins's boots courtesy of
D.I. Courtland, C.I.D.

The Unseeing Eye is a publishing imprint of
AtlanticOmnibus oü
15551 Sepapaja 6, Tallinn, Estonia
www.atlanticomnibus.com

Atlantic Omnibus

ISBN 978-9916-4-0291-7

"The secret of change is to focus
all your energy, not on fighting the
old, but in building the new."

Socrates

Chapter 1

Evil Micra

*H*ELLO; MY NAME is Molly Turner and I am seventy-three years young, but I don't feel it—unless I am climbing steep hills.

An upright, bespectacled figure with pink tinted hair, most days you can see me wandering the roads and lanes with a litter grabber and a black bag ready in my hands.

You see, in this small Gloucestershire village called Hartpury, the A417 runs though from

Gloucester, and you can actually see people just open their car windows and throw out rubbish.

Before I had started my litter clear-up campaign the previous year, the verges had hosted twice as much rubbish, but I realise it's not a thing that can ever be stopped. Each day, the litter I picked up the time before has been replaced by more. At times I imagine someone's peering at me through binoculars and saying, "That's it, lads. The road's clean now, so get down there and chuck out some more waste for the old biddy to clear up. It's our duty. We give meaning to her life."

In a way, my little task did give meaning to my life. I don't knit or crochet or paint or read much, but I do like gardening and walking. It's a somewhat solitary life, the bane of older people in our society, but in litter clearing I felt helpful; felt my existence validated.

Anyway, that day—*that* day—Wednesday, 5th September, with the bright year fading into wear-your-jacket chilly days, I was ambling past the old school buildings beside the A417, and poking at something in the hedge with my grabber, when I heard cars decelerating. It's a busy road where cars don't generally stop unless they're lost, so I noticed it.

A red car had pulled over, the other vehicles now streaming past it. It had stopped by the gate of the field beside the old school and below the woods, a few hundred feet away and, as I watched, a man got out of the car, opened the field gate and went in.

I went back to litter picking. As other cars and lorries rumbled past, I tugged at a bag caught in the prickly hedge. Plastic bags are the worst. Sometimes they fight until their last shred.

Hearing the clunk of a car door, I looked up to see the red car by the gate do a rather dodgy three point turn in the road, and shoot off back towards Gloucester.

A few minutes later I reached where the car had been. Leaning on the gate, I gazed over the green pasture field where nothing stirred except long grasses in the breeze, and decided to call it a day.

The rubbish bag was almost heavily full and that was my general criterion for stopping. Then I spotted a brown fast-food bag almost hidden to one side in the long grass. I unhooked the gate, went in and reached for the bag with the grabber. As it came up, I could feel its heaviness. 'Wastrels,' I thought, assuming left-over food weighed it down. But, when I looked into the bag, the image of tightly packed bundles of cash hammered into my head and made me feel giddy. It was a *lot* of cash.

I hastily dropped the bag back where I had found it.

So. Much. Money!

My thoughts tumbled over each other as I hurried back down road. 'It must be drug money,' I decided. 'Something like that. Not lost, no, definitely placed there on purpose. Some bad guy will be along to pick it up. You don't want to be seen anywhere near it. Get far away!'

But how many cars had passed me in the short time the event had taken? How many people might have glimpsed my actions as they sped past? Because, for a bare moment, the urge to keep it had been there, the thought bright and sharp in my mind, but I wasn't brave enough. Neither hard up nor a wealthy widow, I knew that kind of money could break a soul in bad ways. And after all the other pain in my life I wasn't going to risk bringing any more into it.

I would phone the police when I got home. Tell them all about it, hand the problem to them to sort out. I wanted nothing of it. I didn't own a mobile phone, or I would have called the police then and there.

No sooner had I reached the old school on my way back, than I again heard cars slowing.

'Don't look,' I told myself, but my head moved of its own accord, glancing back for just a second to see a pale blue Micra stop by the gate.

Now I was scared. By very dint of knowing about the money, I had impressed an inescapable dread in myself. "Home; coffee; cookies," I said, reassuring the frightened lady inside me.

5

"Relax, call the police. It's not like you found a body, is it. Pull yourself together, Molly!"

But maybe one can walk in a guilty way because, the next second, I heard slowing yet again and the little blue Micra appeared, chugging along-side me, a big bearded man leaning over to glare at me from the driving seat as the cars behind overtook him and drove off.

The Micra passed by but pulled into the farm driveway a little ahead and, next thing I knew, the man was out and marching towards me like a guided-missile battering ram. I stepped back, hugging the litter bag to my chest as though it were a protective air-bag.

The man, eyes young and fierce in the beard-ed face, demanded, "Where is it?"

"Where's what, dear?" I asked, aware of the tremble in my voice, putting on a pathetic old-lady charade, hoping to appeal to his better nature. "Have you lost something? I can't say as I've—"

Without warning he lunged forward, wrenched the litter bag out of my hands and, in full view of the cars whizzing past and minding their own business, upended the debris onto the path and poked at it with his foot, then went *Huh* and walked back to his car.

I was glad I hadn't been wearing my back pack that day. He might have made a grab for that too, and spilled my snacks all over the place.

'Oh, he was definitely one of the bad guys,' I inwardly gasped, heart pounding with nerves, so glad I hadn't taken the money. But, if that was what he was after, why wasn't it back where my conscience had left it? Had I missed someone coming across the fields; someone sneaking out of the woods where they'd been waiting?

The evil little Micra and its burly driver who fitted it so badly drove off towards Gloucester leaving me peacefully alone, so I put on my latex gloves and scooped the rubbish back into the black bag, knotted its top, then headed home with firm footsteps, halo intact, looking forward to biscuits and coffee and maybe something a little stronger.

'A lot stronger,' I decided as the Micra sailed past again, the bearded man looking at me a fraction too long, the car almost veering across the road as he gave me the evil eye. And five minutes later he passed by on the way back from the village, but I resolutely stared forwards, innocence in my bespectacled gaze as I hurried home.

Chapter 2

Death and Life

I SLEPT WELL that night, but that's the effect of my meds, not that I wasn't worried about my strange encounter, which I had tried to press to the back of my mind. I hadn't bothered calling the police. After all, if the bag was gone, I couldn't even prove I had seen it and, as Ozzy had said, 'If you don't *need* the police, leave them alone.'

So that Thursday morning, I had a good breakfast, then drove Ozzy's car out of the garage onto the drive and gave it the monthly wash. Technically, it's mine now, but I still think of the Mercedes as being his. It suited his temperament: old, distinguished and ostentatious. I kept it in good repair, fully intending to sell it one day and get something smaller. 'Not a Micra!' my wretched mind had to shout at me. But it's nice to sometimes meander down the lanes in the lovely blue Merc and get admiring gazes. I was, to be quite honest, more attached to the car than to the memory of the man who had bought it.

After picking some raspberries from the garden to chill for tea, I fed Misty, my old calico cat, for the third time that morning. Or was it the first time? I would be the first to admit my memory seemed to be slipping a little, the lines blurring with repetition, I supposed. Sometimes I found something wasn't where I left it, so I'd laugh and blame 'the ghost', but I don't think there is one. Not Ozzy's at least; he might well have gone straight to hell.

Having had my elevenses, it was time for my daily wander. I left the Merc on the driveway to dry properly. There's nothing worse than rust to depreciate a vehicle. Ozzy had been depreciated by rich food, dying in his sleep. He'd been down in Bristol for a business meeting, and stayed for a party afterwards. I'd been invited but hadn't gone. His circle of friends was not my circle—and I just didn't like them. He'd complained that I never went anywhere with him and stormed out, and I'd never seen him again. The coffin came back, and the Mercedes, and my long lost freedom was re-instated.

Ozzy hadn't liked me driving—like many things, it wasn't in his world view of women. Does it sound nice to be cosseted and have everything paid for? I know women who envy me, but it's also a kind of prison, especially when your husband won't even let you watch what you want to on TV. And litter picking? Heaven forbid; he would not have allowed that. I could still hear him in my head disapproving every time I left the house, but the walking and the activity, that slight idea of helping the village to keep clean and pretty, were the things that kept me going.

Occasionally I would do different routes, down the side roads as long as they had paths, along to the petrol station and so on, but that day I found myself heading back to *that* gate; in *that* field.

Something had been going on there. The grass was trampled, turned up, scraped about, and I guessed it had been a rather serious game of hunt the very expensive burger bag. Or had the money gone and just the bag was left, empty? The bearded man hadn't specified the circumstances. Someone was going to be in trouble over that. I just hoped it wasn't going to be me, because—as you know—I didn't take it. Or did I? No, I was sure I hadn't, yet that image of the bank notes burned so vibrantly in my mind it seemed for a moment I could see myself lifting them out, looking all around, wondering if anyone would notice...

'You're going senile,' I told myself sharply and got on my way again.

At the edge of Hartpury, a wooded hill looms over the A417 and the old school and the fields, and there's a path beside the school leading up into greenness, where the first brush of autumn painted the leaves orange and red, conkers bristled on branches, and ripening blackberries festooned the brambles.

I went up the path, even finding bits and bobs of rubbish up there, puffing a little as I pushed myself on the steep slope. I wasn't ready to be old. There were many good years left in me yet if I played my cards right; kept taking the medicine. I'm mobile, feel good, and have some money behind me. I am lucky in many respects. I know that. Just unlucky in other ways.

The path opened out into an area of stumps and thin trees, brambles and ferns, and I walked off the trail and into the woods, eating a packet of crisps while looking down through the gaps in the trees at the field the money was no longer in. My gaze went across the A417 and off to the fields on the other side of the road, where my imagination changed the gently moving grass of the field to soft ocean waves.

I had always wanted to live by the sea. Since I had been a child, the call of the sea infected me, beckoning like a siren, but Ozzy was having none of it. I never had a career, having wasted university... but that's another story. I never had my 'own' money, not with Ozzy maintaining my place was in the home, caring for Gavin, doing needlework and cooking and croquet on the lawn—I'm kidding with the last one, but it gives you more idea of what kind of man he was. And, although cloistered, I had welcomed not having to go into the rat race I saw other people stuck in.

My husband's passing had given me freedom from his martinet ways, but no sense of peace. I often wondered if it was best to go quick like that, or to know you have time so you can say goodbye properly, to reflect on the good times—for there had been some—and to apologise for all the things that went wrong, find a feeling of settlement, especially over Gavin—

"Hullo there!" called a cheery voice, and I jumped and turned. A slim, elderly gentleman, wearing a fedora and an overcoat despite the warmth of the day, leaned on a silver topped walking stick, smiling at me from a good-looking neatly grey-bearded face. "Wonderful day, isn't it?" he said chirpily. "Nice views up here." He drew in an exaggerated breath. "Good air, too."

"Hello," I said, tentatively smiling back, morose thoughts slipping away. "The view is nice, but the air? Well, some days when they're cleaning out the barns the air has a real heavy 'country' pong to it."

He pulled a big smile; extended a hand. "Sanderson, major, retired. Pleased to make your acquaintance, Mrs...?"

As I gave his hand the briefest of shakes, a worried little voice asked, 'Where did he come from?'

I know a lot of people in this village, though one doesn't get to see many. Working parents, pensioners off doing Pilates and book clubs, none of it my scene, 'But you don't know everyone!' my suddenly panicked stupid brain yelled. 'He could

15

be one of the bbgs—the big bad guys—missing their money, checking up on you.'

I told my imagination to shut up. This man might simply be new to the area, and there I was, putting him in court with the bad guys, and yet…

"Molly," I said, not offering a surname. "I haven't seen you around before, Major. You new to the village?"

"Molly. Then you must call me Richard," he said, beaming again. "And I live over there, in Highnam." He waved in the general direction of that village over the Leadon valley. "I managed to get one of the older buildings with some residual charm. Even got a wine cellar and a functional well, would you believe. I generally walk in Highnam woods but today I decided I would like a change, so came up here."

A buzzard screamed high above us. They breed here; I've seen their nest, like a dinghy made of sticks. We both looked up at the raptor wheeling above the woods. "Have you seen the red kites?" Richard asked. "There's a new pair over Highnam woods."

"Oh, yes," I replied keenly. "I've seen a pair here, too, though could be the same ones considering the closeness. I *do* enjoy bird-watching. You too?"

"Indeed I do. Flocks of long-tailed tits bringing their broods to the feeders at the moment. Looks like it's been a good year for them."

"Yes, and the swallows' babies are up and squealing in the centre of the village." I was smiling too. Bird watching is a simple pleasure and the idea of shared enthusiasm was relaxing me in his company.

But abruptly he looked at his watch and went, "Aha, I'm out of time. You'll have to excuse me, Molly—business calls." He lifted his fedora in a polite old-fashioned farewell, grinned endearingly and said, "Until next time, my dear." Before I'd even got my *goodbye* out he had marched off down the path, walking stick click-clicking on the stones, and the last I saw of him he was withdrawing a mobile phone from his pocket.

'I am going to have to stop associating everything with that money,' I said to myself. 'There is no reason whatsoever that lovely man had anything to do with it. Just a nice man, out for a walk. Dapper, responsible, respectable.' I hoped we'd meet again. I wanted him to be a nice man I could talk to, walk with, and laugh with. I realised with a sudden pang how lonely I was. The conversation with Richard was the longest I'd had with a human in maybe a week. Age does not diminish your desire for good male company, and I don't mean intimacy, just yin and yang, people complementing each other. It had been just over a year since Ozzy had become not alive. Maybe it was time for me to make another effort to fit in with society.

Until next time.

I had liked that idea.

I walked home over the top of the hill, past the ridge cottages, then down the Old Road's steep slope, past the silent chapel and onwards to the not so silent new school. The playground fair bubbled with children, screams and shouts and laughter reminding me of what I had once had, and lost, and what I can never have again.

Some days I feel I am doing nothing but waiting for the end. The end of my story, of me, of the bad things that torment my mind when I am sitting at home, so I walked slowly, using any excuse to dally and make the walk longer. 'Check the ripeness of the elderberries. Might make some cordial this year. Let's see how the sweet chestnuts are coming along in the field down the bottom. Be nice to have a few for Christmas. So much tastier than those in the shops.'

Upon reaching my cottage, I was met with a piteous meowing. Perched high in the wisteria that half covers the building, Misty was claiming she couldn't get down. I wasn't surprised. She's getting on a bit now, still kittenish in some ways, but at ten years a cat is no longer young. I got her for company when Gavin—

Oh well, she was one of the few things that Ozzy approved of.

As I went to give her moral support, my eye caught a flash of dark blue in the back garden, someone shooting out of view, clothing flapping? A crow flying off? Not a person, surely?

"Oh, so is that why you're up the vine?" I asked Misty. "Did someone scare you?" Misty scrambled herself down and ran off. 'Tea and biscuits,' I thought as I opened the front door. What could be more cheering than Garibaldi and—

I froze in horror.

My house had been ransacked.

Chapter 3

Custard Screams

MY POOR cottage!

Everything was everywhere. Drawers had been emptied, letters and newspapers scattered over the floor like patches of snow, the good cutlery spread around making strange silver graffiti on the rugs. Ornaments sat askew on the shelves and the china in the glass-fronted cabinet sat all lopsided. The settee and armchairs had been pulled out, cushions up-ended, while my precious

21

books lay like dead birds with wings spread on the floor. Nothing but mess could be seen, all the cupboard doors swinging wide; a scene of chaos.

I had a strong suspicion of what they had been looking for.

'No, it's simply a random burglary,' I said to myself, digging under where I could see the phone cable like a snake hiding.

After I had called the police, I tucked the now-dry Mercedes back into the garage while thanking my stars no one had stolen *that*, made myself a cup of tea, then sat in the front room while I waited for the police to arrive. I took the brandy with me, for courage, and the sherry in case the brandy ran out, and I ate through a packet of bourbon biscuits I'd tucked away for visitors because, oddly, the biscuit barrel had also been burgled and all the Garibaldi and custard creams were gone. I'd been invaded by a biccy-scoffing burglar. I wanted to go upstairs to see what might be left of my jewellery, but I didn't want to—what's the expression?—*compromise* the crime scene.

The police turned up eventually, one Sergeant Williams along with a female forensics officer, and by that time I was a wee bit woozy. I'd taken what was left of the sedatives I had been given after Gavin's disappearance. They were well out of date and, in retrospect, maybe not the best things to mix with the alcohol, but they helped me feel calmer.

The police took photos and looked for fingerprints. No one had actually *broken* in. All access points to the house were still locked.

"Does anyone else have a key?" the Sergeant asked.

I shook my head. "No, no one."

"Not a cleaner, a handyman, a gentleman friend?" (I laughed at the way he put it. I suppose I am too old for a 'boy' friend). "Not an ex partner?"

"No one," I said again firmly, feeling I was not being taken seriously.

To my shame, it turned out I had left the tiny larder window open. And somebody who would have to be thin as a catwalk model had squeezed through it, leaving dirty boot marks on the inside frame.

"What did they take, Mrs Turner?"

I had no idea. I wobbled up the stairs to look. My jewellery, some of it gold—Ozzy's apology gifts had often been lavish—was still there in the dressing table drawer, and that made me think again about that money. That had to be what they'd been looking for if they'd turned their noses up at easy things like gold necklaces, and an expensive car on the driveway whose keys were hanging just inside the front door.

So I drew up my bottle-courage as the young policeman and I sat each side of the dining table and I began to explain what I thought was happening. The trouble was, you could tell from his frown that he thought the lady in front of him was crazy. It was quite likely the alcohol on my breath convinced him, not to mention the array of well-sampled bottles on the sideboard. Notes were taken, but eyebrows lifted.

"You did right to leave the bag there," he said in a measured tone.

"Of course I was right, I'm a frightfully honest woman, but the point is they think I didn't leave it. They think I took it and it's here. The BBGs, I call them—the big bad guys."

As he looked at me as though I were mad, the policewoman came in and handed him a note.

He looked up at me with a bigger frown. "The car in your garage, Mrs Turner; you are aware it's showing signs of being in an accident?"

"I…" My thoughts went fuzzy at the change of topic, the strange accusation, the nerves I was feeling. "I thought… I thought I got you here for a burglary. Can we concentrate on that?" I felt my face flush and took off my cardigan to try to cool down.

"I see no evidence of an actual *break-in*, and although the place is a royal mess, you admit nothing's been *taken* except biscuits." He glanced at the bottles. "Are you sure of your facts? Magically vanishing burger bags stuffed with money,

25

mysterious bearded men accosting you, a distinguished looking man chatting you—"

"I never said he chatted me up. I said we chatted. Listen, I'm not making it up."

He sighed. His expression seemed to be blatant mistrust, mixed with old-lady-wasting-my-time fed up-ness. "Why didn't you call when you found the bag?"

"Because the bearded man—"

"So now there's a man with a beard too?"

"I did say that, didn't I?"

He scanned his notes. "No." He looked up. "You'd better start from the beginning again."

I was sure I *had* mentioned the man and that the policeman was double checking on my perceived notion of the truth, so I calmly repeated everything as he made more notes and nodded to himself.

"All right, so back to your vehicle," he said. "Can you explain the damage to the nearside front panel? There was a collision in Corsend Road earlier this morning, and the car fits—"

"Don't be ridiculous!" I declared, getting redder as matters cascaded even more out of hand. "I cleaned it off just today, and it was fine. I don't know why there's a dent in it, but it couldn't be from me driving it drunk."

"You were driving it drunk?" he asked in surprise.

"No!" I took a deep breath and said slowly. "I just assumed that was what you'd been thinking."

He scowled and wrote in his notes again. Probably something like 'old lady is now being snarky'.

I must have been so red by then that I could have been used as a stop light. "I don't ever drive it far. It's a kind of safety feature—a watchdog, so no one will rob the house if there's a car in evidence."

"But you say they *did* invade your house with the car there?"

"Yes, no, it was on the driveway this morning. I put it back in the garage before you came."

"And you didn't see the damage?"

"I didn't go round that side. I reversed it in. I always do. Ozzy—my deceased husband—used to say 'always park for a quick getaway'."

"Getaway? From what?"

"Not *literally*, for heaven's sake. It was just this 'thing' he'd say… " Between the alcohol rubbing my system up the wrong way and the policeman's disbelieving stare I was getting panicky.

"Listen," I said, leaning forwards over the table, trying for sympathy. "Everything I touch turns to trouble lately. My friends don't want to talk to me because I'm so miserable, even the vicar's avoiding my phone calls, and now you won't believe anything I say! I can't stand this. I am an honest woman! Stop making me feel like I'm not."

"Now, now," he said. "We do have counsellors, you know. Shall I arrange one for you?"

I shook my head as the young policewoman came back in. "The driver was ID'd male," she said to the sergeant and swept out again.

"Oh no!" I declared, full of sudden realisation. "*They* did it. Just something else to make me uncomfortable. They—the BBGS. They must've got the keys out of the house, taken it off the drive this morning while I was walking, crashed it and put it back."

"Uhhh… Not too likely, is it, ma'am? But you're off the hook if the driver was male."

I was mashing my hands together, my head ached and I sweated none too sweetly. Was this all connected with the money? I wished I did have it. I'd have given it back in an instant if they were going to frame me for things.

I heard mewling.

"I've got to let my cat in," I said, half rising as the policeman asked, "How many cats do you have?" and his gaze was on Misty, curled up on a nearby chair.

"I thought I heard her at the door," I mumbled, scaring myself with my confusion. "Look, I think you should just go and I'll have a lie down and stop worrying, all right? I do appreciate your coming. Long live the good old English bobby, eh?" I gave a wan smile.

"Anywhere you could stay for a while, Mrs Turner?"

"*Ms*," I said. "*Ms* Turner. I have nothing to hide. I'll stay and sort out, see if anything important's missing."

"And, just to be on the safe side, maybe consider getting your locks changed?" He raised his eyebrows, making it a request more than a suggestion.

I was left in peace to tidy up. They said they'd check in on me later. I suspected it more likely they'd send the social services to certify me, but no one turned up at all.

Now, whether or not Richard the dashing major was involved in all the oddness was anyone's guess, but, realistically, at the speed I walk, I reckon it would have been possible for him to arrange the ransacking of my house, and short theft of car, in the time it took me to walk all the way back. Hadn't I seen him reaching for his mobile the moment he'd left me on the hill? Hadn't I caught sight of someone fleeing the garden as I returned? They'd likely gone through the hedge, over the fence, into the field and run away. That's the trouble with having your nearest neighbour a field away. I could be murdered in my bed (nasty thought) and no one would hear me scream.

How did they know where I lived? I was pretty sure I could have been shadowed by the Micra the day before and not noticed it. Or someone could have asked at the Post Office: Who's that lady who picks up the litter?

However they'd found out, it had happened.

I called the workshop that usually did the car's repairs but they didn't have a space that week, so I booked it in for the next.

I called my car's insurers and asked what I should do about the accident I had not caused. They needed a police report. So there was something else to sort out. Wasn't it Shakespeare who had said, 'When sorrows come, they come not single spies but in battalions'? How right he was.

As the cold evening closed in, Misty came though the cat flap and nestled on me. But she didn't settle, wandering meowing, which is not like her. She was spooked, I reckoned. I almost fell over her as she slunk around the room, doubtless sniffing strange scents of BBGs and police-people.

After baking a batch of cookies to un-spook myself, I settled down to eat said cookies and watch TV, but after all the excitement and the booze, I promptly fell asleep in the chair.

At 02:15, according to the digital clock by the flickering TV, I was woken by a slight noise, and something in the TV-lit room moved. The good thing about wearing glasses is that it's hard to tell in half-light if someone has their eyes open or closed, so I peered around covertly.

A large shape was in the room with me. I couldn't recall for the life of me if I had locked the back door after coming in from the garden, so I was sure I had another burglar. He moved silently around. I faked a snore, trying to stay calm, to not gasp for air. He stopped, then I felt him pass by the back of the chair, go out to the kitchen, then I heard the faint clicks of the back door opening and shutting.

After a moment I got up and hurried to lock the door, heart thumping, wondering what was going on in my life. But the door was already locked and, through its glass panel, I could see in the garden, out by the flower border and outlined by the solar lights of its edge, a figure stood silent and still, just a blackness, no features discernible, though my prickling senses guessed from its mass that it was the driver of the Micra. And he had the ability to get in and out of my house! The key, which I always leave in the door, must have been copied during the first 'visit'.

'Yes, Mr Policeman, I do need to change the locks.'

I went back to the kitchen and leaned heavily on the work top as I recovered from seeing him.

Then I noticed the custard creams.

A new double pack of custard creams had been placed by the biscuit barrel. As an apology—or as a warning that they could get in any time they wanted—I did not know.

Chapter 4

Plants Bite

*I*T WAS EARLY morning on that sunny day called Friday, 7ᵗʰ September, and I was well into the tidying of my violated house, trying to view it as a sort of late summer spring-clean. The door knocker sounded a sharp *rat tat tat* and I answered it to find Richard on the doorstep.

My heart jumped. It was surprisingly nice to see him again.

He took off his fedora as if it were a funeral and said sombrely, "Heard you'd had a spot of bother. Thought I'd come see how you were."

"That's very nice of you, Richard." My heart warmed to him. "Who told you? Is it all over the village already? I hope everyone battens their hatches."

"Indeed," he said. "The coal man said this morning as he delivered: 'Heard that Molly Turner's house got done over yesterday,' he said. He sounded obnoxiously cheered by it. Some fresh gossip to impart, I imagine."

I managed a wry smile. "They couldn't find anything decent to take, from the look of it, or my cat saw them off—she's part Rottweiler."

He laughed.

"Jack-the-coal tell you my address too?" I asked.

He gave a beautifully cheeky smile. "Couldn't resist asking."

I smiled back, though I doubt my smile was as breathtaking as his. "So, coming in for a cuppa, Richard?"

He came in, sharp, intelligent blue eyes looking all over, parked his silver-topped cane in the umbrella stand and sank gracefully into the comfy chintz-covered chair. I made up a tea tray using the new custard creams, buzzing around the kitchen, humming.

"I like that," he said.

"What's that?" I called.

"Reminds me of my late wife," he said, appearing in the doorway. "She would always hum in the kitchen. She liked musicals." Then he added strangely, "Every part of them."

"When did she leave us?" I asked, thinking how a poor lonely widower and equally lonely widow might, just might, make something quite nice together.

"Some time ago." He pursed his lips and looked sad and thoughtful, as though wondering whether or not to tell the story. I decided not to ask but he went on, "She went to London to see Les Mis, never returned, and then I found she had run off with an actor so I divorced her."

I coughed a laugh, not sure if the information was sad or funny. "Oh… I thought you meant she was deceased."

"She is. The rapscallion she favoured over me murdered her with a stage prop."

I stared a moment before gulping, "That's awful."

He gave a lopsided smile. "I call it poetic justice, my dear. Now, where's that tea at?"

"I've only got custard creams," I said hurriedly. "There were bourbons but I ate them all. Had a nervous nibbling session yesterday. That's hardly surprising given the circumstances, is it?"

"Just as well I'm watching my figure then, or I would be offended."

He laughed; I laughed. I wanted to like Major Sanderson, retired. He took his seat again as I brought the tray through and Misty jumped onto his lap.

"Scoot!" I said, reaching for her.

"No, no, it's fine," Richard replied, stroking Misty who purred her approval. I could have purred mine too.

But suddenly the cat sat back and hissed and grabbed at his sleeve with teeth and claws and I had to pull her off. Something flickered deep in the major's eyes. I'd swear another person glimmered in there, sending a tingle of fear into me for whoever I was opening my house to, and maybe my heart too. I should have listened to my senses, but I told myself not to be silly—anyone reacts badly when a cat decides to maul them.

I suppose we ended up telling each other our life stories over tea and biscuits, and what adventures he had experienced! I was enthralled, fascinated, really feeling the atmosphere from this man.

We got to talking about the Mercedes and its delayed repairs, and he instantly phoned a garage who agreed to come and get the car that very afternoon.

"I hold sway in some places," he said. "It's all in the manner. Act grand and they will treat you accordingly."

Almost two hours later, after cancelling the appointment at the regular garage, I watched the

Mercedes being driven up the ramps of a breakdown truck by a young man still in his teens, while I chewed my fingers, nervous of his driving, and waved goodbye as the truck turned out of the lane.

"They'll take good care of it," Richard said, sensing my nerves. "Expensive cars make for expensive mistakes. They are very good with my Audi, though your Mercedes's worth two of mine, I'd say."

Back indoors, he looked out of the kitchen window at the garden's colourful sprawl and said, "I have to take leave of you now, Molly, but I hear there's a sale at Munchkins garden centre. And I hear they make excellent cream teas," he added with a twinkle in his eye. "Would you like to go tomorrow, social calendar permitting? Ten hundred hours good for you; for pick up?"

"Is this a date?" I joked, although my mind said, 'Please, let it be'.

"Definitely an assignation," he said. Then he took my hand and kissed it lightly. I drew away instinctively, hoping he didn't think me rude, but I was still touching it as he left.

In the night, the BBGs decided to empty my shed. They didn't make much noise as everything was carried out and lain upon the lawn bit by bit— mower, strimmer, Ozzy's tubs of random screws and nails, the tool box, the old easel… everything. I stared at it all spread out, bedecked with dew, and tried to tell myself it was yet another sorting thing, something I would enjoy. I wasn't going to let myself get upset, I would turn the negative into a positive, and this time I wouldn't bother to tell the police.

So I spent a peaceful Saturday morning putting it all back in again and finding a couple of things I had mislaid, so it did have its uses. It all proved to me that the BBG thought I had their money hidden somewhere, though I also had to wonder why they were shy of outright threatening me, *we'll chop up your cat if you don't tell us* sort of thing. But I was glad they weren't like that.

I began to wonder if one of them was someone local that I would recognise and that was why they
kept hidden. And gave me biscuits. Odd.

Richard appeared at the side gate. "Ah, there
you are, Molly. I've been knocking on the front
door. Thought you'd come to grief. You need to
get a remote bell."

"Is it ten already?" I sighed. "Sorry, I quite like
sorting things out; got carried away."

The padlock was broken but I latched it
on anyway and hurried inside to tidy myself
while Richard waited patiently. I was only ten
minutes.

"I approve," he said heartily, looking me up and
down. "I like a woman who doesn't fuss around
and waste half a day getting ready—and yet still
manages to look so lovely."

I think I blushed the same pink as the flowery
top I had on over slacks.

On my driveway sat a two-seater Audi convert-
ible, a sporty little blue thing, even more interesting than my Mercedes. I sat in the passenger

seat like a princess with the wind in my hair as we set out on the short trip to the garden centre.

Let me say, it *should* have been short, but he decided to take a scenic route, and go rather fast too, whizzing down lanes with no respect for other cars. We were hooted at twice. Three times if you include the tractor that was so busily getting out of the way that he didn't have time to hoot.

"Do you always drive this fast?" I asked breathlessly, hanging on to the grab handle for dear life.

"Live life the way you want to, Molly. That's my philosophy. Take it by the delicate bits and throw it the way you want it to go."

"Into a hedge?" I asked as we cornered and caught some drift on the wheels. I gripped the grab handle with both hands.

"Scared?" he asked, laughing all over his face. And for a second I felt that same misgiving as I'd had when Misty mauled him.

"Not in the least," I replied cheerily. "It's rather exciting, but I must warn you I might need *two* cream teas after this."

He laughed loud and happy, and slowed the car as the garden centre came into sight.

It was a great day of plant admiring, plant buying and cream cake eating. We were going to go Dutch but he said no, emancipation had its place but this was a cream tea date and he was old school, so he paid.

So it *was* a date. I went quiet. 'Just enjoy what fate throws at you,' I thought, but realising how I had easily resisted the money fate had thrown at me. I really had all I needed by way of belongings, it was just my soul that needed food. If I were to become firm friends with Richard, life might finally be fun. At our ages, he surely couldn't expect anything from me but platonic friendship, right? 'If he isn't a BBG.' How I wished I could quell that blasted little voice.

'Why, if he is a BBG, would he go to all these lengths to find out info?' I asked myself. 'Or is he playing some twisted game with me? Or is he simply an attractive innocent man who seems to like your company, you daft old biddy?'

43

Back at the house, after unloading my new green treasures, and over a cup of coffee, he sat on the settee beside me and told me what a wonderful time he had had and dropped a spontaneous peck on my cheek. I pulled away quickly, his touch on my skin the usual flash of fire I felt at any physical contact. The bane of my life. I smiled to cover any perceived rudeness because I have become good at hiding my feelings about such things, of pushing down a certain memory so I can function. Richard smelled of some male lotion, spicy yet sweet, and I wondered what he would make of my 'terms of engagement' should we get really friendly. Then he ruined the moment by pulling a piece of paper from a pocket and handing it to me. "Almost forgot. The contact for my cleaner: Katarina. I thoroughly recommend her."

My eyes automatically shot around the room. He though it was messy?

He saw my startled glance. "Don't be offended, my dear. I thought, with all the gallivanting we two are going to do, it would be nice to come back to a spotless house."

"Oh, thank you," I said, now in awe of his consideration, looking at what Katarina charged. Not bad if she did a good job. These old cottages could get very dusty.

"Are you alright?" he asked. "You've gone a bit pale. Too much excitement for one day?"

"Exciting day. Definitely. Thank you. See you later," I gabbled, and I felt afterwards that I had pushed him out of the door rather rudely.

Because, you see, my wretched imagination had suddenly decided that Katarina was going to be a spy in this slow dance of suspicion.

Since it was Saturday, I reasoned a house cleaner wouldn't be working, so I called the number on the paper. A young, pleasantly-accented voice answered. She'd been cleaning for the major for over a year, she said. He always paid on time and was a charming man who had said some very complimentary things about me. After that comment, I had to take her on to find out more.

Chapter 5

Tree Tentacles

*T*HE SUN CAME out through the morning mists on Monday, a truly autumnal spectacle. Still curious about Richard, I went to the Post Office and the nice lady there checked on him with her computer. He'd been on the electoral roll in Highnam for three years, she said, so that made me feel better. It didn't seem too likely that he had popped up on the BBG network just to seduce me into revealing the location of a considerable amount of missing money, but something still bothered me.

I wandered back up the path to the woods and sat on a tree stump overlooking the fields and the 'sea'. With that money, if I'd taken it, I could have bought a house by the real rolling and noisy sea.

I sat a while and listened to bird song, and tried to imagine the traffic drone as the waves below me. It was so peaceful,

For some reason it suddenly came to me that I wasn't high enough to do the view justice, so I looked the trees up and down and contemplated climbing one to get a better view. I stepped carefully around a capped well. There are two that I know of, hidden in the undergrowth, safe enough to stand on but the idea of what is below that cap makes me feel ill. Still water and I are not friends. The sea, rolling and passionate, yes, but dark lake/pond/well water, no way.

So why shouldn't I climb a tree? None of us are getting any younger. Why not climb a tree if

I felt like it? I had climbed many in my childhood. It was not like I was a novice. There was no one to see; to laugh at me, but my inner voice tutted, 'And no one to take you to hospital when you fall!'

I told the voice to shut up as I looked around again and spotted a likely candidate.

About six feet off the ground, I looked down and got vertigo. The thin branches hooked in my jacket and seemed to pull at me. I imagined they were either telling me off for my silliness or asking me to stay and play, and I didn't appreciate either idea. So there I was, in the woods, trying to conquer my own reactions sufficiently to get down again, all the while calling myself more names than Ozzy ever had.

The sudden murmur of male voices from the direction of the path was a relief and I shouted, to my chagrin, "Help!"

Two men appeared through the trees, staring at the spectacle of a lady in a tree, hugging it for dear life. The younger of the two, a tall, gingerish man in his fifties, put out an arm to the shorter, greying older man, asking him to stay back as he approached me.

'More spies?' asked my head. 'Get out of that mindset,' I complained to myself. 'You'll end up in a psychiatric institution with full blown paranoia at this rate. They are coming to rescue you. You got that, Molly? *Rescue* your silly old hide.'

"Hi," the ginger man said with an amused smile. "Nice up there, is it?"

"Hello." I smiled back uncertainly. "I think I did a silly thing. Chasing your youth at my age doesn't seem to work. Could you help me down, please?"

I got down with a bit of help then went back to the tree stump for my back pack, litter-picker and black bag. "I was out collecting rubbish," I explained, "when the strange urge to climb a tree overcame me and I foolishly succumbed. I don't know what I would have done if you hadn't come by to rescue me." I took a deep breath, thinking how lucky I was they'd come along. "Would you believe there's rubbish up here too? People are so useless, ruining nice places so pointlessly."

"I was just saying something like that to Dad," he replied. "Aye aye, there's a green bottle poking out the ferns over there. May I…?" He took the litter picker. "Hang on, Dad. Stay here," he said like he was talking to a dog. He nipped into the ferns and returned with a plastic abomination for which I opened the bag's maw.

"I think I could do this twenty-four seven," I said despondently, "and it'd never be ending."

There was something about Dad's demeanour that puzzled me. He was placid, childlike, smiling vacantly.

The younger man saw me looking. "Head injury," he said matter of factly.

"I'm so sorry," I muttered.

"Happens." He shrugged. "Just have to deal with what life throws you, eh?"

He wiped his hands on his jeans and held out a hand. "Callum Bushey," he said as we shook hands. "And Dad is Joe. We live down at Copsely Ridge. Been there a few years now. Seen you walking along the road sometimes, good soul that you are. All the rubbish you must've picked up in your time, you deserve a knighthood or whatever it is they do for ladies."

"Sainthood?" I suggested and laughed. "Molly Turner, patron saint of litter pickers."

We chatted for a few minutes, my infernal internal suspicions dying and drifting away on the wind. Joe was not acting, of that I was certain, and Callum was nice—not as nice as Richard, to be sure—but I felt easy in their company in a way I hadn't for several days. I told Callum where I lived and offered him cooking apples any time he was passing.

I put on my backpack, armed myself with picker and bag, and walked back along the path and along the Old Road with them, chatting cheerfully. Even Joe joined in now and then, although his comments sometimes didn't seem to be related to what was happening in the moment, but when we reached Copsely Ridge, a small cottage rather like mine but with a wonderful view over the Cheltenham valley, Joe suddenly got agitated.

"Is Myrna there?" he asked, his eyes flitting from Callum to me and back again, panic in his poise. "If it's Myrna, I'm not going in."

Callum put an arm around his father's shoulders and consoled him in a touching reversal of roles. "It's okay, Dad. Everything's fine."

I was invited in for a cup of tea. Joe was seated at a table with a kids' thick jigsaw box. Callum tipped out the pieces and Joe immediately began to sort it.

"He's improving," Callum said with a slightly rueful smile, "but they said it'd be a long process." He beckoned me into the next room, a kitchen diner, where he made a pot of tea and took a cup through for Joe, with cookies on the saucer, before we sat with ours.

"Myrna's my ex," he explained. "She pushed him down the stairs."

"No," I gasped. "How horrid."

"She said it was an accident, but she and Joe had had a few run-ins. He reckoned she was a hanger on; like, not pulling her weight financially, buying stuff we didn't need, jewellery for herself, dresses, furniture even. One day I came home and found men moving in a new suite and the old one wasn't six months old. I mean, I do like nice things, but that was a bit much. We argued. Dad came round, we argued more. Then Dad went up to the bathroom and she thundered up after him shouting rather nasty accusations, and then Dad came down ass over tip over the balustrade, smashing his head on the corner of the hearth, and Myrna's stood there with her hand on her mouth going, 'It was an accident, I swear!'"

"Hence the *ex*. I am so sorry."

He sighed. "Been two years now. To be honest, it's been very hard. I can hire carers if I want to go off on my own; work, shopping, whatever, but Joe gets upset if I'm gone too long. And the other reason I don't think it's an accident is because he gets so agitated if I even say her name and… I don't know how to explain this, but he's very *defensive*. I mean, he reacts badly to loud voices."

"It brings back bad memories when he hears raised voices, that sort of thing?"

"Yes," he said slowly. "Maybe. I don't know. I choose to look after him so it's my problem, but Myrna got off scot-free. That's what rankles with me." He took a big swig of tea and looked grim. "Yeah, the authorities actually believed it was an accident. Honestly? I hope she's on the other side of the planet now, because if I ever see her again I won't be responsible for what I do." He looked at me in alarm. "Oh good grief, Molly, I'm sorry. I didn't mean to burden you with all this."

I waved a hand. "Not a problem. It helps to talk about things."

'And your own problems?' I asked myself. No, I wasn't ready to chat about Gavin yet.

I made sure I said goodbye to Joe when I left, and he smiled at me and said, "Bye bye," pointing to the half finished jigsaw.

"Well done," I said enthusiastically. He beamed.

Outside, the sky had greyed and drizzle begun. I released the folding umbrella from my back pack as Callum said, "That was nice of you, with Dad. People don't generally bother once they re-alise how he is."

"Pfft!" I said. "We live in a world where people can't even take their rubbish home. They likely regard him as more rubbish than person. They think things have to have a use; know what I mean? They can't exist just to be nice or pretty."

"Do you have children?" he asked. "I think you must be a great mum with an attitude like that."

He felt the answer in my hesitation.

"Sorry," he said. I just smiled a thin sad smile at him, feeling tears I had thought were all gone welling up as I fought not to spill all my unhappi-ness onto this poor man with the wrecked father.

So I just said, "Make the most of what we have, right? Could always be worse; so many things to be grateful for, if we look for them."

"You're right. It's just finding them that's the problem."

The rain blew off again and I plodded away along the ridge road, remembering what my eternally optimistic father had always said: 'Life is just a series of slight inconveniences waiting for us to deal with them.'

Deal with them? How? Unbidden thoughts of an incensed Ozzy found their way to the light. The old argument; whose fault was it? Gavin's for drinking too much, Ozzy's for not even trying to help him, mine for not standing up for my son and getting him into some kind of programme? When Ozzy threw him out a part of me had died, and when he'd drowned we had spent a lot of time blaming each other.

Maybe all this current madness in my head was because I still hadn't accepted his nothing-ness. Ozzy had destroyed all the photos of Gavin after kicking him out, even the baby ones. So if I hadn't managed to save one, of him in his twenties, all grown up and beautiful the way a son is always beautiful to his mother even when she's adopted him, it would be like I had imagined his existence.

I keep the photo safe in a drawer. Maybe one day I will be able to face having it framed, hang it on the wall, or up on the shelf and smile at it as I pass. But that time has not yet come. He'd have been forty this summer. It's hard when your child has no grave to visit. You could almost imagine he was still alive somewhere, very quiet, very busy, just forgetting to call home.

Chapter 6

Katarina's Talons

*L*ow MORNING sunlight flared into my east-facing front room as I drew back the curtains. The fields across from the cottage were white with dew, the sky flawless as a blue baby's bum, the trees standing high and proud in their late summer finery.

I will admit, I walked into the kitchen hoping my particular brand of fairy had delivered some more custard creams, but there was nothing on the side except a purring calico cat who wanted feeding.

Sat in my armchair while I munched on my breakfast muesli, I turned the TV on to political things, flicked to old and boring programmes, and turned it off, wondering if I should make the effort to drag my old hide into the technological wonder-world of computers and mobile phones, but I had managed thus far without them.

But some days I felt trapped. Yes, I had the car, but it wasn't much more than a beautiful stone around my neck. Even the weekly shopping run was done via my bus pass—would you risk a Mercedes in a supermarket car park? No, I didn't think so. I had friends, but either I had avoided them after my bereavement, or they had avoided me, and now any encounter seemed off, awkward. Most days I didn't speak to a single soul, but I'm happy in my own company most of the time.

Anyway, when people said, 'How are you?' it had faded from being a sincere question into a meaningless token wording. They might as well

just say, 'Hello', and walk on by. Those I had wanted to engage with always felt like they wanted to
escape my conversation, and those who took the
time to talk to me, I ran from in case they touched
on something I did not want to talk about.

Once, I'd even overheard someone saying how
they thought I was odd. In this age, I can be proud
to be odd. It's got to beat ordinary.

In times past I suppose someone would have
yelled *witch!* and got me out of the village that way.
But I do them all an injustice. They have their
lives, I have mine, invigorated only by walking
around picking up rubbish, making myself feel
useful and less lonely. No wonder I was making
a habit of talking to strange men.

❧

At five to nine there was a knock at the door
and I greeted the new cleaning lady, who looked
like a teenager with black curly hair, too much
eye make-up, gold hoop earrings the size of hand-
cuffs and the longest red nails I had ever seen. Oh
yes, she was gorgeous, but looked like she was

going to a party more than a cleaning assignment. How could she clean with those talons? Even her clothes, that hugged her like a lover's grasp, seemed unsuitable for the tasks she was about to undertake. But who am I, Ms Tweed-and-scarf, to comment on fashion?

I paid Katarina in advance then explained how to not lock herself out with the dodgy Yale. I showed the spy, ahem... the cleaner... around and then went off for my walk. When she'd asked for a mobile number in case there was a problem, I again thought of getting a phone.

To my surprise, as I approached the old school, I saw several cars parked up along the roadside and a spread of people out in the field with metal detectors.

Obviously, metal detectors do not respond to polymer banknotes, but my immediate thought was they were being used to cover up the reason for the BBG's searching. I hoped they would find that horrid burger bag soon. I'd had enough worry from its absence.

'Imagine how you'd feel if you had actually had taken it,' I pointed out to myself as I made my way along the path on the other side of the road, ignoring the searchers. "Good luck," I whispered to the pixies of fate. "Let them find it so this is all over. I want to hear a hurrah, a eureka, or something," but no sound came that I heard.

I arrived home just in time to see the cleaner out. She had done a good job. Much though I love Misty, chasing cat fur was never my idea of fun. It gets everywhere. I agreed she could come the next week, same time, and off her ample hips sashayed down the lane to wherever she had parked.

As I turned from the front window, I saw something out of the French doors. A large shape like a hulking man seemed to loom by the shed, but I realised it was just the plastic sheet blown off the cloche, caught on the shed door swinging in the breeze. But the door's movement meant someone had opened it again. Although the padlock was broken, it had held when I pressed the catch in. Since it was now out, that had to mean someone was still looking around my place. Had it been Katarina?

⁓

It wasn't until the evening I realised I hadn't seen Misty since I'd let her out after breakfast. I looked into her favourite places, her trees and hidey holes in the garden and house. I called and rattled the treat bag and checked the shed, but I didn't find her.

'Cats go walkies,' I told myself. 'No need to worry. She'll come back when it's dark, calling for her treats, mooching around the settee, trying to trip me up.'

But, as it got darker, I took a torch to check the road, fearing the worst, full of the horrid sinking emptiness of having lost something else I'd wanted to keep close. And when I got back it was very dark, and I had not closed the kitchen curtains, and there in the back garden I saw a man again. I would swear to it. But I pulled the curtains across forcefully and scuttled into the front room to turn on the TV, loud as I could stand, to drown out my feelings.

I woke at one in the morning, then three, then five. Each time I got up and checked for Misty, calling through the open kitchen window into the black of the garden, shaking her tempting bag of treats. She had never gone off this long before. At five I heard rustling and called out hopefully, "Misty?" only to hear with some fright a deep male voice say, "No."

More than alarmed, I slammed the window shut and hurried into the front room. I should call the police again. Or maybe I had imagined the voice. It was just the one word, after all. It could have been tree branches rubbing in the breeze. How silly would I seem? And if it was a person, they'd likely gone away when they'd realised their error in answering the question without thinking.

I realised it was possible to be totally useless and talk yourself out of any situation.

I didn't sleep after that, just lay awake, praying for the return of a cat, asking forgiveness for hating my dead husband, begging a pardon for not being there when my son had needed me most; you know, all the silliness in life you couldn't control and wish you had. After seventy-three years there are a lot of old miseries you have to push down to act normally.

I realised the days had rolled around to it being Wednesday again, already a whole week since I had found the bag. A busy week full of new things, new worries, old regrets.

So, when the door knocker sounded at about nine in the morning, I dragged on my dressing gown and answered the summons reluctantly and bleary eyed.

Richard stood there, but not my nice smiling Major Richard of the finely cut beard… no, here was a fierce-eyed Richard look-alike who pushed past me into the lounge before he span and demanded angrily, "Where are my diamonds?"

Chapter 7

Horrible Huggy

"WHERE ARE my diamonds?" Richard had repeated angrily.

"What?" I gasped, not understanding the awful look on my friend's face. "What do you mean, Richard?"

"You will refer to me as Major," he said coldly. "And you know perfectly well what's going on, old girl."

He stepped closer.

I stepped back so my waist touched the dresser. I tried not to look scared. I had stood up to Ozzy. I could stand up to this peculiar man.

"We have searched *everywhere*," he said, "and there's no sign of the diamonds, so I know you must have them."

"The only diamonds I've got are in my engagement ring," I snapped.

"Oh… feisty, aren't we?"

"I've been let down by someone I thought liked me," I complained. "Of course I'm going to be angry. Perhaps you'd care to explain just what's going on?"

"The burger bag."

"There weren't any diamonds in *there*," I blurted before I caught myself.

"So, you finally admit it?"

I sighed with heavy acceptance of my idiocy. "I saw the bag; yes. I saw the wads of cash in it too, but I didn't touch the money so maybe there were diamonds underneath the wads, but I wouldn't know, and don't ask me where that blasted bag is because, when I saw what was in it, I dropped it back exactly where I had picked it up like hot coals."

He *hmmd*, watching my face closely, seeing the hand pressed to my wildly beating heart.

"Any danger of you having a heart attack?" he asked.

"No. Why? Do you want me to? Fall down and die? Let it do your dirty work for you?"

He laughed shortly. "No, Ms Turner, I am actually, despite myself, quite fond of you; of your spirit. I just want to know how far I can push you to tell me where my diamonds are. If you had a heart attack, I'd never know, would I?" He stepped closer still. Scrunched up against the dresser, the drawer handle dug into my back.

"Go away," I said, "and leave me alone. I swear by all that's holy I saw no diamonds in that bag. The beardy man—the one who grabbed me and spilled the rubbish out of the bag. He must've told you I didn't have anything."

"Ah, yes, him. The fat prat. The new help." He thought for a moment.

"What did you think of him?"

"In what way?"

"Was he thorough? Did he search *you*?"

"I… I don't like where this is going."

"His name's Huggy. I hear he likes to hug people. Hug people really hard, until they can't breathe."

I shuddered. "So…? You're going to make him squeeze me until I give you …what? Lies? Because that's all they can be."

He nodded slowly, the soft blue eyes I had liked so much becoming cold marbles that made me feel unwell. "I think we'd best search your house and grounds *again*, Ms Turner. I can face losing the cash—it can be recouped quickly enough— but the diamonds?" He shook his head.

"Are you sure the diamonds were even in the bag to start with? Maybe you've been double crossed by your own kind."

He looked down his nose at me for a second, and I could tell he was considering my suggestion. "No," he said. "No, I'm sure that's not the case. So, as I was saying before you so rudely interrupted, I've already spread it around that you're having some work done on the house, so the neighbours won't be surprised by any comings and goings. Huggy will be your house guest for a few days, to keep a constant eye on you. A distant relative, perhaps?"

"Well, there's definitely trolls on my husband's side."

"We will take this house apart brick by brick—"

"But you've searched already, and the shed, and I bet your 'cleaner' had a good nose around too."

He smiled wanly. "Katarina—"

"She *was* a blinking spy!"

"More than that. The lovely lady is my wife."

"Mail order, I assume," I said. "So why'd you go on a 'date' with me?"

He laughed. "Obviously, I thought you might let slip the truth of you and the bag. Come on, don't you watch spy movies?" He glanced out of the French doors. "I think we might dig the garden too, while we're at it."

"Oh, goody. Can you get the potatoes up?"

"Your humour is barely humorous."

"I've nothing to hide, Major. How about you dig the whole garden, just to make sure?"

"So they *are* in the garden?"

"Oh, good heavens," I cried in exasperation. "I keep saying, I haven't got the fecking things!"

His eyebrows went up. So did his cane in a threatening manner. "I had hoped you would see sense, Ms Molly, for I am a reasonable man and you are an honest woman, but if you need more encouragement, I can offer it." He waggled the cane.

I drew in a breath and said, one word at a time. "I. Don't. Have. Your. Diamonds."

The cane smashed down on the coffee table, denting the corner, sending a sliver flying off. I jumped and put my hands up before me.

"So it is to be the total house search," he sneered. "You stupid woman. You will regret it. I don't make a habit of beating women, but I could make an exception in your case if I don't get what I want. You understand?"

71

I nodded feebly, he moved away, but he stopped at the front door and looked back, his eyes travelling up and down the tatty towelling dressing-gown I wore. "If I were you, I would get something on; maybe a suit of armour, before Huggy gets here. And we have your cat."

That did it. "Threaten me if you have to, but not my cat, you horrible little man!" I raged, my fists bunched. "How could I have ever thought I liked you? Taking a defenceless, innocent cat, hostage? If you hurt her there'll be hell to pay even if I have to come back from hell to mete it out myself!" I wanted to thump the truth out of him, trembling so much my heart started hip-hopping.

But he simply frowned, shut his mouth on some comment, and left.

I dressed hastily. A thick woolly jumper and denim trousers were pulled on as my cloth armour, not knowing what to expect from the horribly named Huggy.

But when he arrived, walking through the front door as if he lived there, having used some manner of master key—I shouldn't have been surprised—he grunted something then went to the kitchen and helped himself from the biscuit barrel, turned back as an afterthought and took the whole barrel, then sat heavily on the settee, munching.

"Coffee," he said, not looking at me. "Two sugars, don't scrimp on the milk. Cream if you got it."

"Yes, sir," I said as sarcastically as I dared. He didn't look up, so I risked a curtsey too, but he didn't care, leaning over to grab the remote off the coffee table and turning on the TV, flicking through to the sports channel and football. Oh my, that was going to be worse torture than having my house ripped apart.

"Do you know where my cat is?" I asked.

"Hmmm," was the absent minded reply with both eyes on the TV, then he suddenly leapt up shouting "*Goal!*" as he punched an arm into the air. It shocked me so much I fell back against the dresser.

"You okay?" He looked down at me from his wide height then offered me a crumby hand.

"Get lost," I said as I refused his offer and struggled up. "I'm not having any catnapper touching me."

"I haven't napped yer moggy," he said, frowning offended and slumping back in the chair.

"And I haven't got those damned diamonds he's on about. People are assuming things left right and centre, aren't they. When's the demolition crew coming?"

"They're not gonna demolish your house. You know that, right?"

"You know what I mean. Can we go for a walk or something? I don't want to be here to see them mess it up."

He shrugged, looking morosely into the tin. "Any more biscuits?" he asked, and then, "Where's me coffee, woman?"

"You do not speak to me like that." I glared. "Maybe you should buy some *more* custard creams."

He blinked. "How'd you know it was me?"

"I guessed and you confirmed it. And is it you who's been lurking in my back garden? Trying to scare me? Well, you succeeded. Hope that thought makes you happy. Scaring old ladies indeed! Where *are* your mann—"

A knock called from the front door. I went to open it, dread in every fibre of my trembling body, my knees feeling like they might give way.

Chapter 8

Sharp Needle

ALLUM AND Joe stood on the doorstep. "Oh," I said, taking a moment to calm down from anticipative panic mode, thinking their timing was awful, "have you come for apples?"

Callum pulled an embarrassed face. "Actually, I'm after a favour. Could you look after Dad for a few hours? I could tell he really liked you yesterday. If it's not too much of an inconvenience, you know, 'cause this work's come up in town and it's too late to get another carer today. The new bloke walked in and completely forgot what I'd told him about tone and said *Come on, get your boots on, Joe*, in a voice like a flamin' foghorn and Joe went haywire— Oh, gosh, sorry, didn't see you had a visitor."

"Just a relative," I said, hurriedly dismissive before Huggy could say anything. If I'd thought this through, I could have written a note, passed it to Callum... No, there was still the hostage Misty to consider. "Of course," I said brightly. "Joe's welcome. Is he triggered by bangs, though? I'm having some work done on the house today. Or did you mean for me to come to yours? I can't."

"I was going to say mine, but here's fine, and he's okay with bangs. I'm so grateful, Molly. I can't afford to lose this work. In you go, Dad." He pushed Joe into the house and made a quick getaway.

Joe stood just inside the door on the *Welcome* doormat and looked around, blinking as though the light hurt his eyes. I didn't have any puzzles or games of any kind for him, so I was about to take him into the sunny garden to find something to amuse him when the door banged open onto the doorstop.

Ah yes, this time it *was* my 'builders' or 'disassemblers', or rollicking nutcases depending on how one felt about the situation. I moved Joe aside and the troupe of four solid young men in paint-spattered blue overalls, really looking the part, walked in without even saying hello and went straight into the dining room with forbidding-looking tool boxes at the ready. I eyed the big van sat outside my gate with Vanker's Building Works neatly emblazoned on the side and changed it to wankers in my disrespectful mind.

Then I realised who one of the youths was, and my heart sank. He was the same youngster who had driven my Mercedes onto the repair truck. So they had that too; poor old metal beastie. Was it also being ripped apart in the search for diamonds and cash?

I steered Joe into the garden, not wanting to know what was going on indoors, picking up the fat-ball bucket on the way and filling the bird feeders while Joe stood and watched and seemed to want to eat one too.

Huggy, appearing from the kitchen with a slurping great mug of coffee in his hands, set it down on a side table and moved to the chintz chair to watch both the TV, and us in the garden, and the lumpy, scraping, thumping song of furniture being shifted began. I hoped they didn't damage anything in the dining room. There were many pieces of Lladró china, collected over the years, and some exquisite Waterford crystal. But what could I do to protect it? I had never felt so vulnerable.

I flicked into another gear. "Can you help pick the apples, Joe?" I got two baskets from the shed and handed him one, and soon had him putting the apples in it as I handed them down from my perch on the ladder.

Huggy came into the garden.

"Who won?" I asked out of habitual politeness.

He took a rosy apple from Joe's basket, bit into it, chewed once then spat it out.

I tried not to laugh. "They're cookers, Huggy."

"Huggy!" cheered Joe, doubtless hearing the word *hug* as an invitation, dropping the basket and flinging his arms around the startled man, who pushed him away angrily. I saw a sudden dangerous spark in Joe's eyes and calmed it hastily with a delighted, "Well done, Joe! You're doing a really good job. There's more on the little tree, over there."

As Joe walked to where I had pointed, I cornered Huggy and said, "Joe's got something wrong with him, so be nice, you hear? If you want to be useful go and pick some blackberries." I gave him a big old margarine tub and pointed at the brambles. He looked at the tub then the brambles with little recognition. I took him to the hedge. "Green berries bad," I said like I spoke to a child. "Red better, but black nice. Okay?"

He began to pick them.

Joe was now by the pond, poking at the fish with a cane from the runner beans' support. It appeared that between the first time berry-picker Huggy, and Joe the fish tormentor, I had two children to educate.

"Where're you from, Huggy?" I asked when I'd managed to entice Joe back to apple picking.

"Nowhere," he replied.

"Is it a bad guy thing; that you don't talk about families?"

"Ain't got one," he replied as he popped another blackberry into his mouth and continued gathering them.

"I had a husband," I volunteered. "He died suddenly. I have no children. I do have a sister called Lottie but I lost track of her some years ago."

Lottie had hated Ozzy. Said he was bad; that she could sense it. Looking back, she'd had the right idea, but I had been young and in love and foolish, and I had screamed hateful things at her and sworn I'd never talk to her again. And now I had no idea where she was. Maybe, when all the weirdness was over, I would buy something that could access the power of the internet and see if she was—

"He's at it again." Huggy indicated Joe, pond-paddling in his socks.

As I grabbed Joe, sat him on the bench and stripped off his sodden socks, it reminded me of little Gavin and how I had been an awful mother, unable to help my child. And Ozzy had been a worse father.

"Why d'you bother with him?" Huggy asked, watching Joe with a sneering not-understanding as I rinsed the socks under the outside tap and draped them on the washing line.

"Why not?" I replied. "He's someone's dad. He's loved. Don't I have a duty to care for someone else's loved one when they're in my care?"

"Right," he said thoughtfully, then, after a second of gears whirring. "What food does cats like best?"

"My cat liked fishy food."

"K." He went off down the far end of the garden, got out his mobile, and I heard his low voice in a muffled way, but one of the words might have been *fishy*. I hoped that meant he did know something about Misty, and that she was okay.

I spent the rest of the morning with my two boys… haha. Huggy was pitifully keen to learn everything about the garden. You'd think he'd lived in a cave all his life. While the workmen investigated my rooms and seemed to be having a really good time, laughing as they turned my life inside out, Huggy, and even Joe, listened as I pointed out the edible berries in my wild hedges, and the inedible ones, and tasted and spat out the ones safe to try but better cooked.

I was just wondering what to feed them for lunch when Callum returned and took Joe and his wet socks away with many thanks. Just outside the door, Joe called back, "Bye bye, Myrna. Rot in hell!" with a cheery wave which dampened any hopes of a future in child-minding.

"Got chips?" Huggy asked.

83

"Umm, are there any in the freezer? Do I have to feed the other lads too?"

"Nah." He waved a hand. "They'll be off to the pub in a tick." He stuck his head in the chest freezer and poked around. "Bit empty. Peas, sweetcorn, frozen sprouts… bleurgh. No chips." He straightened up. "Box of eggs on the side here."

"Okay, I'll do egg and chips. There's potatoes in the garden. Could you be a dear and dig up some for me? It's my back, you know; aches a bit after digging. I really need someone to help me with the heavy stuff nowadays."

"Taters?" he queried as though it were a foreign word. "Spuds? What? I asked for chips."

"Which are made from potatoes."

"No way!"

I stared at him, unable to believe such ignorance. "You want me to show you? Go get some. Three big ones, like your fist, and I will demonstrate the magic that is cooking."

"Great." He rubbed his hands together then went to the shed for a fork.

As he dug the potatoes, I glanced across to the small coven of plants waiting in the corner to be planted out—the plants I had bought from Munchkins while on a happy date with a man I had thought liked me. If I was a vindictive woman, I'd have chopped them up and fed them to the compost, but that's like hitting your children when your husband has abused you, just passing on the pain to no good end.

⸺

As the evening darkness crept over the garden, Huggy started to look at his watch repeatedly. The lads had stomped off and gone in their van just after four. Despite their short foray to the pub, they had eaten almost everything in my kitchen—except the Brussels sprouts—and I was hoping they'd bring their own food the next day.

"Are you my gaoler tomorrow too?" I asked Huggy as he sat on the settee where a dent showed every time he stood up. "If you are, could you do some grocery shopping before you get here? Otherwise we'll both starve. Much though I adore your company, when are you leaving? Or do you have to tuck me into bed and read me a story?"

He snorted. "Oh, very funny, Ms Tur—"

"Just call me Molly."

"Nah, too close-like. Ms T. How's about that?"

"All right, but what about tonight?"

"You tread careful tonight." He looked grave.

"Because?"

"'Cause I'm gonna go when Needle turns up and takes night shift."

"Needle?"

"That's what we call him. Needle, 'cause—" He caught himself. "Yeah, so he's the guy got through yer window. He's that thin, y'see."

"So he's not as nice as you are?" I asked.

"Bloody hell," he said, taken aback. "Don't let anyone hear you say that. 'Specially the major. You're supposed to be scared of me; scared I'll hurt you if you put a foot wrong. He tell you why they call me Huggy?"

"You like to hug people *hard*."

"Yeah, but I don't *like* it. I do what I'm told."

"So… so… oh my." I backed away, a sudden cold fear enveloping me. "Seriously, have you killed people by squeezing them?"

"Nah, Ms T, they just pass out, but it's right scary and it helps get them to talk, you know, if someone needs some info. Just got shoved down this backwater from London. Ain't hugged no one here yet. Don't even know me way around the place. Too many trees."

"But… you're not going to *hug* me, I hope?"

"I don't want to, but if the major asked I'd have to. Reckon he's not asking in case, like, you're fragile and you pop all over me Doc Marten's before you talk."

I raised my eyebrows. "So old age does have benefits."

"You do see, don't ya? I don't wanna hurt you."

"I find that reassuring."

"But if he asked and I didn't, he'd do me in, 'cause I wouldn't be useful no more. That cane of his, it's a swordstick, and I hear he's fond of using it. Nasty."

"I think you're all terrifying," I declared. "You're like a swarm of wasps sitting on me, and I'm just waiting for one of you to sting me."

A gap appeared in his beard as he chuckled. "I like you, Ms T, and don't tell anyone *that*, neither."

"So, if you like me, please tell me where my cat is."

His smile fell. He had just opened his mouth to reply when, without warning, the front door opened and the most cadaverous man I had ever seen in my long life crept in like Gollum, mousey hair long and lank, eyes big and round and cold as a shark's.

"You! You keep out my way," the skeleton ordered me with a pointy finger like a Halloween hand. "I wanna watch the movies. Got Netflix? Prime? Sky?"

"No internet here," Huggy said, up from his settee-nest, backing away towards the door.

I vanished up the stairs. Now there really was something in the house that I instinctively feared.

Chapter 9

Bloody Nails

*F*OUND THE un-builders had been in my bedroom. Just a cursory inspection from the look of it, nothing particularly out of place, but I could tell. I checked on Gavin's photo nestling safely in the drawer. The jewellery seemed to be all there, too. Maybe that would change when they had given the place a complete search, like they had in the dining room where I was happy to see nothing had been broken but, as far as I could tell, a few pieces of china were missing. I doubted that complaint would get me anywhere. Besides, it might annoy the lads, and who knew what they were capable of when riled.

Maybe this wouldn't be so bad. Maybe, once the major had been convinced there was nothing of his in the house, they would go away and leave me alone.

Later, when I went down for a glass of water, Needle lay with his feet up on the settee, fast asleep, TV tuned to the horror channel muttering dire things to itself.

But as I went into the kitchen his grating voice called, "Tea, no sugar, milk, any cake you got, crisps, crackers."

"Huggy ate it all," I replied as I went back out with my glass of water. "Gaolers should provide their own food."

He was up and had a hand round my throat before I could say another word. I dropped the glass with a thunk on the rugs, the horrid depths of his eyes defeated me and I whimpered a not entirely fake whimper. He let go. "Behave your fucking self, you fat old broad."

'Well now,' I thought, not showing my contempt, 'this one's very practised at being a BBG.'

I grabbed some tea towels and swabbed the wet rug in silence, threw the cloths into the washing machine then stuck my nose in the air and went back to my bedroom with a fresh glass.

Sat in bed, reading a thriller with a heroine in a much more dire predicament than my own who was coping quite well, which made me feel better in a way, I tried to turn off the fear-switch inside me and relax. But the whole scenario was so exhausting it wasn't long before my eyelids drooped.

I woke to a hand squeezing my left breast through my nightie. I supposed it was Needle but I didn't wait to find out. I did what the heroine in the book had done; I flailed madly in the near dark with my fingers bunched so nails would scour skin. They contacted, Needle fell back swearing loudly then scarpered. I rummaged in the tall boy's top drawer for the internal door key and locked it, as common sense should have dictated to start with.

I trembled. Then I cried from the shock. I felt so totally vulnerable and alone. I knew almost everyone in the village, but just knowing someone doesn't make them a friend, and I didn't need all those people who gave me empty sympathies. I had brushed them all away—maybe because I didn't want to admit how little I had cared that Ozzy had gone, when I knew people who still mourned their spouses.

Even if I had dared to run, the BBGs still had Misty, and she was the one creature I loved most in the world. I would tolerate all this chaos, put up with all they threw at me, so that one day I could get her back safely.

So I lay there in my no-longer-feeling-safe bed, and shuddered and cried great sobs of unfairness, wanting to wash off the feel of the cold invasive hand, resolving to get drinking water from the basin in the en suite in future, even though it always tasted odd, and maybe setting up a little store of food in there too.

I didn't venture out of my bedroom the next day until the workmen, and Huggy with two bags of shopping, arrived at nine. I decided I would not even offer to pay for them, on principle.

And the presence that had been a scratched-face Needle flitted out of the front door like a spectre.

I got Huggy on his own and didn't waste any time in telling on Needle. He looked at me with his upper lip rising in disgust.

"I'll tell the major. He don't like that sort of thing from the lads."

And when I thanked him it was from the bottom of my heart.

⁓

But, and I am sorry that this story is full of *buts*, but things lurched from worse to worse.

A short while later Huggy's phone rang and he answered it. His eyes danced to me and away. Then I heard one of the louts' phones ring too,

93

and a premonition came over me as the atmosphere in the house changed.

"Huggy?" I asked. "What's going on?"

"Sorry," he muttered, and legged it as the louts swept in and grabbed me.

Yes, they grabbed me. Three sets of strong young smelly arms held me back into the comfy chair while the scrawny one with the mean thin face produced a small pair of scissors. He began to cut my nails, hacking at them as I struggled because they were hurting me, reducing my only weapons to not-nails, skimmed to the quick and bleeding.

"That'll teach you to mess up our mate," the cutter said as he stood up, and they all laughed while I suppressed tears and said, "I can see you're a criminal because you'd make a lousy manicurist," and the cutter waved his hand at me in a *get lost* kind of way.

"Come on, Jimmy," the one who had a bushy ginger beard said as the cutter dallied then leaned over me, hands on the arms of the chair and said, "Remember this, old lady. You bite, we bite back harder." Then he went away and I could breathe again.

I got up shakily and went to track down Huggy.

He was leaning against the apple tree doing something with his phone and tried to run when he saw me.

"It's all right," I said. "It's only nails, they'll re-grow."

"You ain't mad at me?"

"Course not. I asked you to tell on him. I just didn't know the major—I suppose it was the ma-jor who gave the order—would react like that." I gave him a close-to-tears smile. "I had worse from my husband, if it's any comfort."

"Your old man hit you?"

I sniffed back a tear. "Not exactly."

Funny how what a man agrees to one min-ute, he is willing to change when it suits him. Ozzy made me certain promises. He signed the pre-nup on the dotted line, well aware of my no-touchee problem when we married. I had thought I'd found safe refuge, but he kept wanting to change the rules.

The house phone rang.

"Leave it," Huggy cautioned.

"Are you sure?" I asked. "It could be important. The car insurance, or urgent scammers telling me my non-existent computer has a virus."

He huffed and muttered, "You'll have to risk it Ms T."

But not half an hour later there was a knock on the front door and, when Huggy peered out stealthily through the curtains, it was a policeman. Silence had descended on the house. I imagined the louts holding their breaths.

"What do you want me to do?" I whispered.

"Get rid of him," Huggy said.

"Oh my, I hate to think what that means in your line of business."

"Quit with the flappy mouth," he snapped. "Just make excuses. Get him gone."

I took a deep breath, opened the door a crack, saw the policeman who had interviewed me, and gave my best smile. "Why, hellooo," I said in my most charming voice. "I'm *so* glad to see you again, Sergeant Williams. Or may I just call you Willy?" I leaned against the door jamb in what I hoped was an old lady seductive way, making sure my butchered nails were hidden. "I'm sure you'd love to come in and have a drink, wouldn't you? Plenty of fun to be had here, I can assure you."

"Umm, no thank you, Ms Turner," the policeman said, frowning, stepping back. "Just, you didn't answer your phone, so I was concerned."

"Gracious me!" I was genuinely surprised. "So you've come to check on little old me. How *lovely*, but I can assure you I'm fine." I pushed my chest out and looked him up and down. "Just *fine*." I smiled again.

"Um, good to hear," he said. "Go careful with that booze, Ms—"

"Please, dear, call me Molly." I winked.

Something like horror crossed his face as he hurriedly backed off, turning away as I stepped back onto the doormat and shut the door, fumbled my way to the settee and took some big breaths of calming air.

"Don't you ever make me do that again," I complained as Huggy stepped in from the kitchen. "That was heart-attack-inducing scariness. Lying to the police? I am a disgrace to the British monarchy."

"That was fucking great!" Jim said from half way down the stairs, the other lads smiling behind him. "I changed my mind about you, Moll." They all laughed and I went to the kitchen and on out of the back door, into the damp garden, girding myself with boots and rubber gloves, ready to deal with mockery and the fear engendered in me from my little act with the policeman, by burying them metaphorically in the ground under the new plants.

I'd just finished planting up the shrubs when Jim ambled into the garden, swigging a can of beer. He glanced around then said something to me I didn't quite catch. When I asked him to repeat it he marched over, pushed my back to the apple tree and grabbed my—you know—that part of me through my trousers and I was instantly enveloped in panic mode and screamed and struggled while he muttered something about old pussies. Luckily, Huggy had heard my yells and came out like a shot and, to my amazement, punched Jim to the ground.

"You okay?" Huggy asked me.

I nodded and said, "Thank you, Huggy," and sat there at the base of the tree all folded in on myself as Jim got up holding a hand to his face and skulked away looking daggers at the pair of us.

Huggy followed me around the garden like a lost dog after that. I asked if he fancied mowing the lawn and a flicker of excitement came to his eyes, but he wasn't interested as soon as he found it wasn't a ride-on, and he was strangely quiet so I guessed he might be feeling a wee bit guilty over my nails.

"It's all right," I said to him. "Honestly, come on, be a chatterbox again. I need the talk to calm me."

I put a reassuring hand on his arm. Big mistake. The louts had been emerging for a break.

"Going clubbing t'night?" Jim was asking the chunky one.

"Yeah, that hot chick'll be there. The one you shagged in the toilets, right?"

"Quit dicking around."

Chunky sniggered. "Maybe it's you that should quit with the dick."

It was at this point he had glimpsed my hand leaving Huggy's arm. "Oh, here's our newbie, a fuckin' granny lover," he sneered. "Huggy loves granny dry snatch."

I felt Huggy tense beside me before he snarled, "Strikes me, the way he's been carrying on, s'more like Jimmy boy here what fancies her."

Jim laughed aloud, the others joined in with the laughing, but Jim's eyes went mean and feral and, when they rested on me, I had to turn my gaze away until they moved farther away, wrapped in their smoky aura.

"Are they right in the head?" I asked Huggy very quietly. "Are they always like that? Do they enjoy it? Is it the way they were raised or something?"

But Huggy strode off into the house, and the louts looked at me and made obscene gestures that made me all the more determined to stoically take whatever they sent my way; to not let them win on any front.

Of course, fate had other ideas about that.

I was trembling deep inside. I could feel it like a subtle vibration and I didn't like it reminding me of that time—the time I had locked away deep inside and only let Ozzy see. The time that had steered my life off the path of study and almost certain success into illness and depression and, eventually, into a marriage of more convenience than love.

"I need to get out of here," I muttered and went to find Huggy. I thought it was funny how I had to hunt for the man who was supposed to be keeping an eye on *me*. He was in the dining room, leafing through a book on nature. Maybe I had sparked something in him. I could see tadpole images on the open page.

"Hey, bookworm," I said, as cheerfully as I could muster. "Can we get out of the house for a walk?"

"Reckon." He shut the book with a clap and shoved it back in its gap on the shelf.

"Okay. Do you want to see some frogs?"

He looked up, eyes widening. "Real ones?"

"Yes. I don't imagine plastic ones would be very interesting, would they?"

But, after trudging across the field, we found the bit of land adjoining the river was very muddy; too muddy for our shoes. We went back home and I dug out Wellingtons from the shed, finding both mine and the ones with Ozzy's initials stamped on—O.M.

"Too big," he complained, shaking his booted foot. I braved the house to see if I had any socks his size and returned to find him looking rather guilty, putting back screwdrivers onto the wall rack as if he'd contemplated stealing them then changed his mind.

"You can have any of those tools," I said. "I never use the things. The socks too if you like, and the boots."

"Wouldn't mind borrowing a few bits and bobs, now you mention it," he said, pulling on the thick woollen hiker's socks I had brought down for him. He dragged the boots on over them and grinned happily. "That'll do it, Ms T."

At the boggy borders of the River Leadon, I took him across to the rocky place where the frogs lived in the day and we lifted stones carefully, finding frogs, toads, and some tiny newts hiding there. He was laughing like a little kid as a slinky newt trickled through his fingers.

Then he stood and said, "I really likes you, Ms T. I bet you were a great mum."

I gulped, bit the bullet, and in a few painful words explained how my drunken son had been lost to the river.

He went very quiet, his thoughtful gaze back over the river, looking as if he had a similar story to tell, but then he sighed, muttered, "I'm sorry, Ms T. Really I am." And that was all I had ever wanted anyone to say.

On the way back, by the big lonesome pine, we met one of farmer Brand's free range chickens who had mastered escapology. We managed to corner her and I showed Huggy how to hold her. She was used to being caught so didn't struggle, and he stroked her with a kind of fascination as she gave slow *chuurrs* of approval.

"Lovely," he said. "Feathers are right soft."

I stroked her too and the memories flooded back—Gavin and the chickens, and the ducklings, and the butterflies and the worms and all the other little things he had loved, and all the heartache rushed back to me and I realised I was trying to replace him with this overweight BBG.

Chapter 10

Marsh Thing

T WAS STILL light, so we walked to the pond and stopped to watch the wild ducks paddling.

Huggy leaned on the railings betwixt pond and road and said, "Shoulda brought bread for the ducks. They like that. Right?"

"The fish eat it more than the ducks." I pointed into the clear water where small fish had gathered, anticipating food from the world above.

"Stupid man," I said, thinking distractedly. Huggy frowned at me. "Not you, Huggy; that major. What does he think an old lady like me could do with his blasted diamonds?"

"Take 'em to a pawn shop."

"Seriously? Just like that?"

"That's what he does... I think. Where else d'you think he'd fence them? Buck Palace?"

"Well, I wouldn't know, would I?" I said tartly. "How big were they, anyway? What's all the fuss about?"

"I dunno," he said. "Weren't mine. Even tiddly ones are worth a bit if they're nice and clear."

"And how many were there?"

"Crap, Ms T, you're asking the wrong bloke. Not my thing; pretty rocks. Now, cold hard cash, that'd do me fine."

～

Don't let anyone tell you the countryside is a quiet place to live. Apart from the ruckus the ducks were making, there were rooks and jackdaws calling noisily overhead, there were several mowers working up the road, a hedge trimmer chattered, cars came by constantly, a light plane zoomed overhead, and over the other side of the field a small JCB chugged as it cleared out ditches in preparation for winter.

Then a big yellow combine rumbled past us, first the main machine then the header pulled by a tractor. Huggy looked on in awe as the massive machines trundled past us almost within touching distance. "I'd like to drive something that big," he enthused. "Looks cool!"

I couldn't think how to divert his 'career' in that direction. "Look it up on the Internet," I suggested. "If you don't look into things you'll never find a way of getting out from under the major's boot."

The combine vanished up the road. The small JCB in the field fell silent, the ducks settled their argument, the mowers stopped, and a black cat paced over the now quiet road and vanished into the hedge.

I sighed. "I wonder how my cat is."

Wordlessly, Huggy flicked on his mobile then handed it to me. A video was playing; a happy little calico cat being tickled by a laughing black lad.

A tear sprang to my eye. "She's okay! You could have told me *you* had her. I've been so worried. The major wouldn't hurt her, would he?"

He shrugged. "I weren't s'posed to tell you, and anything's possible with that 'un, but I'll try to keep her safe. George, me roommate there, he and me take turns looking after her. What's her name?"

"Misty."

"Like you? Ms T?"

"I never thought of it that way."

"Why're you a Ms anyway? You was married, right? Though you ain't got no ring on." He put the phone away.

"Went back to my maiden name when Ozzy died. Took off the ring because I didn't miss him. It seemed appropriate at the time—new leaf sort of thing.

"You weren't happy. What went wrong?"

My mouth twisted as I wanted to tell, to spill out the whole disastrously captive marriage, but I didn't want to tell Huggy. I shook my head.

"Look," he said, sounding apologetic, "it ain't gonna take too long, then he'll be satisfied you haven't got his stuff and you'll be left alone."

"Not bumped off because I know too much?"

"Doubt it."

⁓

We continued our walk, me wondering how much doubt there was in 'doubt it' and chatting about the merits of owning cats—if one could own a cat or if the cat owned you—eventually coming to the church and its graveyard.

I went to Ozzy's plain granite-chipped grave and looked down at it, considering how helpful he might have been in this situation. He was certainly good at shouting, wheedling, persuading.

Huggy looked down at the inscribed headstone, then said, "Oswald Marshman."

"Yes. My husband. I changed my name when he died. I didn't like the surname. Marshman—I ask you! Like a marshmallow, all sticky-sticky. Or a monster that comes out of the marsh all nasty oozy mudness. Marsh Thing. It's the sort of surname that leads to kids being teased."

"Bad name, yeah," Huggy agreed.

"My son should have been buried here too."

"Where's he at then?"

"No one knows. The river goes to the sea, the sea goes to eternity. His body was never found." I hadn't wanted to say those words. Not those specific words: *never found.*

I glanced at him. Under the beard it was hard to tell how he felt, but he folded his hands in front of him for a moment as though giving reverence to the dead, then he said, "I'll give you a moment then," and walked off a little distance, reaching for his phone.

❧

So I stood there and thought of Ozzy and tried to not think of Gavin while Huggy kept a respectful distance. Then he finished with the call and came back, motioned for me to follow, so I did.

Back in the house, it was instant mood reversion; Huggy back to watching TV and pressing buttons on his phone, while still wearing Ozzy's boots.

"They're comfy," he said to my questioning glance. "And you said I could keep them."

"Mud on the carpet?" I asked.

"Nah, look, you could eat yer dinner off 'em. Washed 'em under the outdoor tap while you was taking yours off."

I shrugged. What was a little mud compared to the dusty chaos of the rest of the house. I watched his thick fingers dance expertly across the tiny keyboard of the phone. "I don't get the attraction of those things," I said. "Waste of time."

"Wanna play a game?" he asked.

"What? No." I laughed. As if I did that kind of thing. Games on phones, ha!

"Look." He waved it at me. "All you gotta do is move the little yellow light to bust the coloured rocks with the gun. Easy, right? Bet you can't beat my score."

111

An hour later, I was sat hunched up beside him on the settee, still battling Rock-Popper, and had learnt so much from him I felt humbled.

We were learning from each other. Maybe replacing missing elements of each other's lives. If it wasn't for the sounds of people ripping my house apart for something they couldn't possibly find, I could have felt contentment in that time. I had also resolved to buy a mobile phone when it was all over.

A spicy smell wafted around the house. The lads were upstairs and I dared to go up to see what was happening as Huggy went to make coffee.

In the jumble bag in my wardrobe, the monsters had found a raunchy red and black bustier. It hadn't been mine. I'd found it when sorting out Ozzy's stuff. It had likely been purchased for one of his women, but now Jim was wearing it and prancing around like a moron. An effect of smoking the weed I had smelled, I supposed, though, it being Jim, it might have been just the way he was hardwired.

I folded my arms and stared at him in disdain. "Suits you. Brings out the red in your eyes."

"Oh darling," the stupid youth lisped. "I am sooo ashamed of myself. I have been a *very* naughty girl; you must spank me." He turned his chino-clad rump towards me and wiggled it as the lads roared with laughter.

"This is not funny," I said stonily.

"Yeah, it is!" they laughed and laughed more.

"This funny 'ere, then?" asked Jim. His hands dived into the top dressing table drawer, lifted my one and only photo of Gavin that sheltered there, and shook it at me.

"Give me that!" I ordered, grabbing for it.

He swept it away. "So who's this, Moll? Eh? Speak up. No shame in having a boyfriend, and you like *boys*, don't you?" And he tore it into four before I could do anything.

Incensed, I scrabbled for the pieces as he let them fall. Could I glue it together again? I clasped them to my chest and glared at Jim to voodoo him dead.

"Ooh, you done it now, Jimmy boy," ginger beard chortled. "Gran's gonna have a right paddy."

I stomped down the stairs, tears pricking my eyes, went into the back garden through the French doors and sat on the bench still holding the pieces of the picture like precious flakes of gold.

Huggy appeared a moment later, worry on his face. "Thought you'd done a runner. Don't scare me. He'd have my hide."

I rounded on him. "Seriously? You didn't hear what was happening upstairs? You could have stopped them, couldn't you? Just walked in and said *stop*?"

He looked seriously confused. "Well, yeah, but no. I couldn't do nothing. It don't work like that. It's a higher-archy."

"Hierarchy! Honestly, sometimes I don't think people even try to better themselves." He looked pained and then angry

"All right," I conceded. "I know there'd be no point complaining to Major Nitwit. Not that

I imagine he's a *real* major, not really. With him being all highfalutin and posh and pretending every day. How can you do it? Do what a man like that says?"

"Don't shout at me." He glowered.

"My one and only picture of Gavin, my darling son, was torn up in front of me."

"But I didn't do it, you mad old bat, so calm down."

"And who's brought in weed?" I demanded. "I know that smell from times past. I don't want that in the house, the beer and cigarette stench is bad enough. Tell them to get their fingers out, quit messing around and get a move on."

"They wouldn't listen to me, that's what I'm telling you. Come on, Ms T, get yer boots on and we'll go down the river again. I know you like that."

I stared at him then put the pieces of Gavin's photo carefully into my handbag.

"Consideration at last, Huggy." I managed a wan smile. "There might be hope for you yet."

But a storm came on, so we sat in the Micra and played on the phone, and peace descended on me for a vague measure of time before the lads left and we managed to find food in the house and watch TV while gluing the photo back together.

"Ere, I know that bloke," Huggy said unexpectedly.

"My Gavin? How?"

He lifted the resurrected photo and peered closely. "Yeah, that's the bloke. The woman called him Rocky."

I felt my heart do a funny flutter of remembrance at the pet name. "Yes, he did call himself Rocky when he was a boy," I said as disbelieving excitement rose in me like the edge of a tsunami. "He had fancies of becoming a boxer, you see. Where'd you meet him?"

"Didn't meet him. At a pub in Bristol last summer—"

"No… you must be mistaken." I could have cried. "He passed nearly ten years ago."

Huggy stared at the picture, his face twisting as he thought hard. "Nah, Ms T. It was him. That's my gift: I'm good with faces."

"But, Huggy, I told you he fell in the river and his body—"

"Was never found," Huggy jumped in. "And no body means he might not be dead. Listen, we was in the pub, the Battleship Royale just off the Bermin Road, and suddenly there's female-type whiny shouting and this woman is laying into her bloke, saying *that's your trouble Rocky Smith, you don't think*, and I saw her all blonde and pretty and him, this bloke here, all cross he jumps up and passes right by me, like, but—"

"Don't! Please, no more. It can't have been him."

A chaos of mixed ideas enveloped my brain: alive or dead, pubbing in Bristol or drowned? Rocky *Smith*? What was going on?

"But, but... *Why* would he do that? Not come home. Not contact me?"

"I don't go home 'cause me old man would kill me."

"Ozzy disowned him, which is extra tough when you've been adopted, I imagine, but I loved him and surely he loved me too. How can I ever find out the truth? The not-knowing is the worst. Afterwards—because this horror has to end eventually—I'll get on that Internet and investigate Rocky Smith for myself. Just how many men are called Rocky anyway?"

Huggy had searched on his phone. "Bad news." He showed me the scrolling list of Rocky Smiths. "All this lot's from a social network site."

I sat back in the chair. I had to accept I might never know, but for a few happy minutes I had thought finding Gavin might be the one good thing to come out of the chaos.

Chapter 11

Fire Demon

*T*HE NEXT morning brought more to worry about. No surprise there.

After the disgusting Needle had left, and the un-builders had sloped in, Huggy paused on my front doorstep as though he didn't want to come in, and when I looked at him I gasped. His face was bruised, one eye puffy, lip cut—the face that had lost the fight. He only glanced at me, his face grim yet his eyes beckoning, before stepping back into the front garden. I went out too, leaving Jim and one lad wrenching my TV unit off the wall, while the other two found something else to rattle about upstairs.

I sat beside Huggy on the bench, reaching to turn his face to examine it, but he pushed my hands away. "Quit fussing, woman."

"Oh god, Huggy, you can't expect me to not be concerned. Who did this?"

He hesitated but couldn't stop his eyes flicking house-wards, so I guessed. "Jim. Because you hit him, right? Because of me."

He put his hands together and leaned forwards, but didn't reply.

"So it's my fault," I said. "Sorry. 'No matter what I do I always get someone hurt."

"Nah…" He sighed heavily. "It's okay, Ms T. Chicks dig scars, bruises, missing teeth. This ain't nothing. Been stabbed before. Had a week in wiv the nurses."

"How gruesome. I think I'd prefer not to know your history after all."

I felt guilty. He'd been defending me and now his face looked like it had gone a few rounds with Tyson.

"Got summit for you," he said.

"Garibaldi? Custard creams?"

His meaty hand swam into my vision and offered me a phone. "For you."

"What?"

"I gone and got you a phone, so we can play Rock-Popper together." He looked very pleased with himself.

"I suppose you want payment for it?" I asked, heading inside for my purse. The food he'd bought had been a necessity, but the phone would reasonably cost a bit. But—surprise surprise—in the handbag hung on the coat peg, my purse was devoid of cash, the bank cards missing.

What do you expect when your house is full of thieves?

I extended the handbag's shoulder strap and wrapped it tightly around me. No way was I ever letting it out of my sight again.

"Never mind," Huggy said when I told him.

"*Never mind*?" I echoed, full of righteous anger.

"I mean, you can keep the phone, no charge."

"So kind!" I growled. "Where'd it come from?"

He shrugged and I sighed. "Suppose I'd better cancel my cards before the monsters bankrupt me. No doubt they have ways of getting round the PIN codes. Permission to call the bank, sir?"

He harrumphed; I went indoors to call the bank on the house phone and wailed about losing my cards.

I did manage *not* to say they were in the wallets of some rogues in my bedroom. It would have made me sound like some kind of prostitute.

That done, I went back out to the bench and flicked through the phone Huggy had handed me and found photos of smiling children. "So you had the nerve to want money for a phone you'd nicked?" I exclaimed. "Just when I think you're half decent you pull this stunt?"

He shrugged, offended. "Leopards and spots. It's a good phone, Ms T, but it ain't really a phone no more. I took out the SIM so you can't call any-one on it, not even emergency."

"A phone that doesn't phone; how useful."

"I put the games on it for you."

"You went out of your way to steal some poor soul's phone just so I could play games with you?"

"Thought you'd like it," he sulked.

I stomped out to the driveway with Huggy hurriedly following me and eyed the evil Micra. "Give me the keys," I demanded.

"Nah," Huggy said indignantly, frowning. "I ain't giving you my keys."

"You stole a phone for me to play with," I said in a low hiss. "And I'm sure it ruined someone's day. Now you don't want me to steal your car, you see what it feels like? And someone stole my car and bumped it, didn't they."

"Weren't me, and no one drives my baby but me," he said, patting the bonnet. "But I'll take you for a run if you want."

"And just who was it took the Merc and pranged it?"

His voice dropped low and he vaguely indicated behind him. "One of them lads. Not saying no more. He—the Major—he just wanted to scare you."

"As ever. Calculating bastard." I hugged myself and pouted, thinking I wasn't going to be able to shame Huggy into becoming a good guy and rescuing me.

—

I suffered through the banging and dust and not-so-delicate moving of my belongings from one place to another. Rubbish and washing up, the grimy untidiness of an abandoned house, filled the kitchen. Beer cans appeared in random corners and I tutted as I moved things around, trying to keep a semblance of order in a muddled house. The place smelled like a pub before they brought in the no-smoking rule. The toilets both stank of men who could not aim straight.

Then they began attacking the kitchen so I wasn't allowed in there. No access to kettle or fridge or bread bin—

"Don't let them defrost everything in the freezer," I begged Huggy.

He went into the kitchen. I tried not to listen to their uncouth voices using expressions I didn't for the main part even understand, then Huggy came back munching a Cornetto. He waved it at me as I made a *heaven help me* expression. "These are good, Ms T."

"So, I needn't worry about the food getting defrosted, just eaten." I threw up my arms in despair. "How can I do anything?" I demanded of him as he sat back in my/his TV chair. "These louts are practically uninstalling my fitted kitchen. I am starving. That obnoxious Jim—"

Huggy shot up and grabbed my arm which shut me up, and he pulled me away. "I know, I know, but be careful what you say, Ms T. Come on, I got more stuff in me car if you're hungry."

His Micra, such an innocent looking evil car, sat outside obediently. I got in, he squeezed in, definitely needing an upgrade—a promotion or whatever—or simply to steal a bigger vehicle.

He finished off the Cornetto and drew out a long vacuum flask and two mugs from a bag in the back seat. "What's this?" I asked. "Slow poison?"

He gave me a *mad woman* look. "Brandy-coffee. Figured you might need it."

I chuckled. "You're an angel."

"No one ever called me that before."

"Can't you get out of this business?"

He was quiet a long moment. "Not much in the job market for someone like me. Can you imagine me cv?"

"What did you want to be when you were little?"

He gazed at me then, his bruised face holding a look so full of remorse I wished I'd never asked the question, so I said optimistically, "What've you got for an old lady to eat, then?"

"Battenberg," he said, reaching into the bag and placing the cake on the dash.

"One of my favourites."

"I know. I got the idea from a receipt o' yours I found."

"Oh," was all I said, reflecting on how he'd been prying around, of course, and my home was no longer my castle. I hoped they didn't steal too much from me. My truly precious stuff, my diamond engagement ring, the house deeds, Will and so on, were in the bank.

Brittle, tinkling crashes issued from out of the front door. I grimaced.

Huggy fished a penknife from his jeans and sliced the cake into two, handed the smaller part to me in its wrapper and scooped up the rest in his meaty hand, munching on it like a hamburger.

Suddenly I realised how much he ponged. The leather jacket he wore smelled of stale tobacco and even staler man sweat, so I suggested we went back to the seat under the front window. Coffee and cake on the garden table, I listened as various bangs and crashes and curses emanated from the cottage.

Gretchen Murr, a nearby neighbour I quite liked, came up the path to us. "Having some work done, I hear, Molly."

"Oh yes," I smiled. "You can definitely *hear* I'm having work done."

She laughed, her eyes flitting questioningly to the hairy man I sat beside.

"Lottie's daughter's boy," I said. "Had a wee car accident." I hoped that was enough of an explanation for his poorly face, but Sarah pressed on.

"And Lottie is?"

"My sister, so I suppose that makes Hugo here my grand-nephew? I never was much good with family trees."

"Me neither, but—"

One of the un-builder's dashed out of the door and barged past her on his way to the van. "How rude," she said loudly, looking to me for an apology.

I shrugged and smiled sweetly. "Young people. What can you do? It's all there is nowadays; rush here, dash there."

"Hmph," she said. "Still, must get on. Can't dilly dally all day. Bye bye, Molly; Hugo." She finger-waggled a wave.

With her out of earshot Huggy said, "Oi! The major been talking 'bout me behind me back, has he?"

"What *do* you mean?"

"How do you know me name's Hugo?"

"Is it really? I just used the first name that came into my head. You know, Huggy does sound a lot like the nickname of someone called Hugo, doesn't it?"

"S'pose." He swigged his coffee, finished off the cake and sat back saying, "How come you're so cheerful, Ms T?"

"Am I?" I thought a moment. "I suppose it's because I'm getting on and aware that I could drop dead from natural causes at any moment, just like my husband died in his sleep. But don't doubt that I'm scared. Yes, I'm really scared, deep down. There are worse things than dying and all this messing up of my life is a horror. I wish I had never seen that blasted burger bag, which I didn't take, and that's all there is to it. I picked it up, I saw what was in there and I dropped it

129

back in the same place. Why's that so hard for anyone to believe? I am quite innocent," I emphasised, "and this is going to be a story where the innocent survives."

I said it bravely. I didn't want them to grind me down. For all I knew, Huggy-Hugo could be playing good cop, but I doubted he had the wits for it. I wondered what crimes he had committed in his time, what possible future a man like him could find.

"It's alright, Ms T," he said after a moment's deep consideration that saw him staring into the distance as wheels turned in his head. "I believe you."

"Thank you, Hugo," I said, feeling sheltered by his words, but I should have known fate would spoil that moment of happiness. Ginger beard ambled out, turned and looked at the upper windows and said quite calmly, "The house's on fire. Sorry 'bout that."

I suspected a joke from his monotone voice, but then the other louts exited much faster, spinning around to look up, and I stood and saw in horror flames licking up the curtains in the spare room above us. "Shut the front door," I said loudly, but no one moved from their spectatoring. "Keep it contained," I said angrily and managed to shut the door despite Huggy trying to hold me back. Damage limitation was foremost in my mind, dulled by panic, my thumping heart, the shaking and nerves and jelly legs of a woman about to lose everything.

"Don't just stand there, call the fire brigade! Get them here fast!" I gibbered as the louts just stood and stared like my blazing house was a firework display. Then I heard Huggy talking to the emergency services on his mobile.

We stood back farther as sparks flew out of the chimney like swarms of fireflies.

I lost it. I totally lost my cool. "Did you do that on purpose?" I screeched as I grabbed Jim by his clothing. "Did you torch my house on purpose, you scum?"

He pushed me off violently. Huggy caught me before I fell.

The flames had a grip. We all ran to the lane and I watched helpless as the crackling hiss became the roar of an animal eating my house. It was a blessing Misty was 'safe' elsewhere, a double blessing the repaired photo I treasured resided safely in my purse, and even a triple blessing that the Merc was in another place.

But the sirens sounding from the A417 and the crackle of the fire hid my impossible to repress sobs.

Chapter 12

Dark Well

WHEN ALL THE fuss was over, when the louts had done a runner and left Huggy and me alone, the house was just a dripping, smoking square with a roof bent and buckled, held on by splinters.

The fire had taken hold quickly and zoomed from room to room, so only the fire brigade's swift response had left anything recognisable. It had busted out through the windows and scorched

the wisteria to a skeleton plant, bounced its fat
fire around the furniture until it was naught but
black wood, smashed the china as surely as ham-
mers, and flame fingers had read all my beloved
books into ash.

"Still got yer hubby's boots," Huggy said quietly, stood beside me out in the lane as we watched
the firemen efficiently go about their jobs. "Don't
tell me you want them back 'cause me Doc Marten's were in *there*."

"Oh Hugo, I can't tell if you're trying to make
a joke to cheer me or not," I muttered. "Keep
the boots. I don't care. Where do you live? Can
I come and bug you for a few days?"

He gave a dull chuckle. "That'd give the neighbours something to talk about."

They were out there now, my neighbours, some
gawking, some walking up and passing by, watching the fireman as they rewound the hoses. No
one had offered help or even the standard British
cup of tea that cures all ills. I leaned into Hugo.
He put an arm round my shoulders. He was the

first man I had let do that in many years, and I didn't care what anyone thought.

"I guess I'll have to find somewhere to stay for a while. That little hotel on the Newent road, maybe. The major can't want any more of me now the whole house has gone, surely? Can you keep Misty for a while, until I get sorted?"

I heard a familiar tapping and, "Well, well, well; what have we here?" asked the major, swaggering up.

"Did you arrange this?" I said with venom in my voice. "So help me—"

"Botched work," he jumped in. "No malice aforethought, I assure you. My fault entirely for hiring those undisciplined idiots. Molly, you can come spend a few nights at my place. Katarina would love to see you again."

"I'd rather not," I said sharply. "I'll find somewhere for myself, thank you very much."

He leaned towards me, eyes sharp and forbidding before saying, "Yes, you will come to my place. Don't think this is over."

"Crap, man. Just leave her alone," Huggy said, moving in front of me. "She ain't done nothing. She's just a nice old lady."

"Huggy, what happened to your face?"

"Had a disagreement with the lads; bit like this one. You hurt her, I'll break your fancy stick over your head."

"Oh?" The major lifted his swordstick, glanced behind him to the positions of the firemen, said, "This one?" and before we could move he whacked Huggy across the head with it so hard he fell, and I jumped back in angry surprise.

The major looked down at the man holding his head then at me.

"Do not run or call for help, Molly," he cautioned in a soft voice. "You'll only get someone else into trouble. Now, Huggy; you've had a disagreement with me too. I brought you onto this team for your subtle skills, so you work to my beat, not your own." Another look at the firemen and another whack as Huggy tried to squirm out of the way. "Not your day, is it."

Calming, the major pulled his coat around himself, tidy and upright, every inch the respectable gentleman again. "The car's parked by the pond," he said. "Walk there now, Molly. Peacefully take my arm, act natural and try to smile, because if you don't I will use the other mode of my swordstick on your friend Huggy, and I can assure you it will hurt him a *lot* more."

～

Less than a half hour later I found myself locked in a dark, cold, windowless cellar, with naught but a bucket for company. Loud rock music played continuously to annoy me, and I had nothing to sit on except the tiled floor. My shoes and handbag and glasses had all been taken, but I could smell something bad and was sure it was old blood.

The room was vaguely circular, and in the centre was a low brick wall that was also circular, the functional well the major had spoken of that happy day in the woods that seemed so long ago. I dropped a loose piece of tiling down it to hear the splash, and it wasn't a long drop to the water, though I may have misheard the splash in the cacophony of sound that vibrated painfully in my ears. I ran my hands over the bucket support, but I wasn't going to feel any farther for fear of unbalancing over the low wall and falling down. And it was the well that stank, oh how it stank, like corruption, rotten, diseased.

The music cut out, light flashed in as the door opened, leaving me blinking. The major stood there, just staring at me.

"I don't know where anything of yours is," I said with a fed-up sigh in my voice. "I wish I did, to get this over with, but I *don't!*"

"Hmm… we'll see. Four days without water. Enjoy. Or I could get Needle to try the heroin on you. You might talk that way. Which do you prefer?"

I was speechless for once.

"There's a bell up there." He pointed to the button. "Ring it when you're ready."

And with that he was gone, and I was alone in the darkness and the music returned, even louder, so the walls and floor vibrated and everything made me feel ill.

I investigated every little corner again. I fell over my bucket and cussed and yelled and screamed at the music. I wondered if I stood very, very still, I could meld with the wall and become invisible, but it was my tired mind playing tricks on me again.

I rang the bell, hoping at least it would shut off the music. It did, but the major was not amused. I had disturbed a meal for nothing. After that I rang the bell and disturbed him several more times, for fun, for five seconds relief for my ears, but on the next occasion he hit me across the head with the stick. Hell; that hurt.

The major leaned on the door jamb and folded his arms over the stick. "Did you know," he began, and I wondered what amazingly inciting detail he was about to impart. "My Katarina, has she told you about that last night, at the dinner after the business meeting in Salveston Manor?"

"The night Ozzy died? No, what of it?"

"My Katarina is beautiful, desirable, no?"

I blinked. "Are you saying not so subtly that she and Ozzy had relations?"

He chuckled. "Relations. Such a nondescript word for casual sex. Very much so, behind my back too. Naughty Oswald; naughtier Kat. I know I cannot satiate the minx—"

"Yeuk; no more verbal torture, please. Not that I believe you anyway. I can't imagine Kat seeing anything in him. What was she there for anyway?"

"Maybe it was because he didn't see anything of *you* on that side of the marriage," he countered. "Had that occurred to you, Molly? I knew Oswald well. He said you were an ungrateful woman. He said all you ever did was complain. Now I've met you, I must say I see his point. You are entirely self-absorbed. Think about that while you enjoy the music."

The major left. He didn't know that I hadn't cared what Ozzy did. Much leeway been signed for on his side of the premarital agreement. Mine simply said that he could never have a sexual relationship with me.

I married a man who would be my saviour, and I would be the pretty thing on his arm who would turn my face from his many dalliances. It had seemed a great idea at the time.

∼

The door opened, the lights flashed on as the music cut off and Katarina crept in. I hoped she'd brought food, but she hadn't. She closed the door behind her softly until just a shaft of light illuminated the room.

"He leave you here until you tell," she said softly. "I know his ways."

"Why didn't he do this first?" I asked, feeling the lump on my head. "This is what I would have expected, not the gradual destruction of my home."

She shrugged. "You are old lady and he wanted to be… gentle. He imagine you give in easy. But Huggy tell him you were Oswald's wife—"

"Widow," I cut in. "But what's Ozzy got to do with this?"

"You pretend still? You did not know? He was my major's boss."

I sank back to sit on the floor, head pounding, a kind of final puzzle piece clicking into my mind. That was why Kat and the Major had been there the night Ozzy died. They were in the same business. The monster! The unutterable monster I had married. The Marsh Thing was real! Keeping me in the dark for years. Me in my sacred gilded tower while he dealt in... I assumed it was drugs. No one had actually said. But if I hadn't hated him before, I did then. Trying to keep me safe had done the exact opposite.

And Hugo, there he was dropping me in it again, though he'd likely have been punished if he hadn't told. What a horrid system to live in.

Her head tilted a little as she read my face. "You did not know. Interesting. My major, he wanted to get stuff gently, but now he knows you were Marshman's woman he thinks you are good at hiding—that you were taught things by him, so he do this hard way. Tell him, old lady. You want to exist here until death? You die from lack of medications? I know old ladies take a lot of medications."

142

"I am *not* an old lady and I won't die without my meds, but not having my glasses is a bit of a nightmare and my head is killing me. The bastard hit me with his stick." She was staring at me with a frown. "Someone will look for me, Katarina. People don't just disappear."

A slight rueful shrug lifted one shoulder. "All the time they disappear."

"He should have tried this to start with," I said bitterly. "Then he'd have soon discovered I don't know anything, and my house wouldn't be burned to the ground and—"

"It is not his style. The burning. I doubt he had hand in it."

"But if the louts hadn't been there, the accident would never have happened, so he's still to blame, isn't he? What *do* you see in him?"

"He is my husband. I do what he tell me, as you did with yours, no?"

"Ha!" The dumb innocence of her broke my heart. "I did that for years, young woman, and believe me it won't get you anywhere. Ozzy could sleep with anyone he wanted to; yes, I let him. It was an agreement we had."

She looked baffled, and suddenly I was telling this bruised flower how I had been broken, and she was nodding in sympathy as I explained the attack, the STI, and the subsequent damage that had blighted my life since my teens.

She rubbed a hand across her nose. I think she was sniffling. "You…" She sighed again and I heard the hurt of years in it. "You nice old lady. You deserve better. I tell you, my major, he is scared to hurt you. Hurt me, yes, because no one care about me, but you? Marshman's widow must have many, many people in the organisation who care about her…"

'I do?' I thought in surprise. That was news to me.

"…so he wants only his diamonds; you give them, all okay. But you don't give them…" I saw her shrug. "…he keep playing with you, like cat with mouse, but he dare not hurt you too bad for fear others hurt him worse."

The door opened. The major appeared, his features shadowed by the bright light, a vampire coming to feast on my innocent blood. "Kat, Kat, Kat," he said in a tired voice. "You should not be here. More dissent in the ranks? What is my world coming to? Leave!"

As she passed him he grabbed her arm and said, "I will deal with you later."

Jim and Needle traipsed in after him. Needle handed the major a cat basket. Misty saw me, cried out to me, turning round and round.

He attached the basket handle to the bucket winch and, even as I saw what he was planning, I was up and the lads were holding me back as I screamed.

The winch creaked, the basket could be heard shaking, the cat's terrified *mewls* echoed up the well, then were silenced.

The major looked at me, no emotion in his gaze. I now saw his little grey beard was the beard of Satan himself, and the horrid louts were demon attendants. I had no words. Nothing I could say would save Misty. There was no truth to tell and a lie would soon be found out.

He turned the handle and the basket was raised from the water. Misty called to me, I sobbed, he lowered her again, watching me, my wretched old face contorted with grief.

I sank down, limp against their grasps, and began to choke as my heart finally complained enough to black me out.

Chapter 13

Rotting Corpse

T HE SHOCK of hitting the cold well water brought me around to full comprehension. Light glowed from on high, the bucket rope was tied around my waist and I was still clothed, but my bare feet found oozy mud and sticks beneath them and I wanted to scream myself out of the nightmare.

Then a hand touched my shoulder and I uttered a high pitched wailing cry, a pure full blooded terror enveloping me. The hand was black and rotting, attached to an arm, maybe once attached to a body. It was bones I stood upon too scared to move, my toes sinking into the vestiges of a corpse.

His face looked down, then Needle and Jim's joined in, the unholy trinity of demons gazing at their terrified victim.

"I am not sure," I gasped, spitting out the vile water, "what you think this is going to achieve." My teeth chattered so much I could hardly speak. "I h-h-have collapsed once, and I'm likely to c-c-collapse again and drown."

"No begging," Needle observed. "No *mercy, mercy, I'm just an old lady!*"

"No denying the charges either," Jim said.

I reasoned there was no point anyway; they didn't believe me. They would never believe me. I could pretend to show them where the stones were, but then there would be no stones and it would all go round and round and…

I thought of dear Misty, a victim of this monster who had his elbows leaning on the well wall while he watched me like a Roman inspecting a dying gladiator.

I thought of darling Gavin, a victim of the man he had grown up calling Daddy, drowning drunk one starlit night in Bristol.

I thought I was going to be a victim too. It might be easier to let go, wait for that time when I would feel warm and drift off as my body heat was sucked out by the frigid water. Feet lifting out of the mud, I did a desultory doggy paddle, heard voices receding, the lights went out, and I was left in the darkness with only loud rock and roll and a corpse for company. "How'd it work out for you then?" I asked it, and I was so far gone I wouldn't have been surprised at a reply.

I figured I wouldn't last half an hour. Confusion came on quickly. If you ask me what I remember most it was the odd lights that sputtered in the darkness, the vile scent of the corrupted body, the odd illusion that I could hear Misty purring in the rhythm of the music, and I said softly, "I'm coming, Sweetie. Mummy's coming."

Then I was out on the floor and choking while Needle and Jim looked very concerned. The major had gone, and I guessed I was not supposed to actually drown or they'd get into trouble. As it was, I thought I was likely to be poisoned by the water.

"Oi. Moll! You still with us?" Jim asked.

"No," I said.

"Huh. Got some spark, this 'un," Needle said.

"I haven't got the diamonds, boys. Please believe me," I begged, my pride almost gone.

Jim shook his head. "Not us you gotta convince, Moll. He'll be pulling out your toe nails soon, since I cut your fingernails too short, you see, so can't get the pliers on them."

"Just chuck me in the well again," I groaned.

"So tell us where these fucking diamonds of his are," Needle said. "I have never met a broad as dumb shit as you. That's all he wants. You wanna die for them? What good's that? You's dead, you can't use them."

The major swept back in. "Any luck, gentlemen?"

"Listen!" I said as fiercely as I could muster. "Just because I was Ozzy's wife doesn't mean anything. He managed to keep me in the dark for years, and I hated the man in the end and it was wonderful to hear he'd died. There, now I've said it. I blamed him for everything wrong in my life; my lack of friends, for persistently trying to renege on our pre-marital agreement, the death of our son, of refusing to adopt any more children—everything."

"Fascinating," the major said, though he couldn't have looked less fascinated if he'd tried. "Is that it, Molly? Yes? Good. Jim, go find me a hammer."

Jim gave Needle a look that I couldn't read. Confusion?

"What?" the major roared. "In my day it was a good thing, a mark of confidence, of acceptance into the group to be asked to get the hammer."

He glanced at me, a strange smile curving his lips. I hated to think what he saw as I lay there hugging myself, teeth chattering, my clothes stinking and wet, my hair muck-matted.

The louts did not move. "What's got into you two?" he demanded. "I have had enough of this stupidity, both hers and yours. If she still won't tell after a little light hammering you can dig the grave; and I can tell you, lads, there is no higher honour than *that*. I was the fastest digger in my group."

I sniggered at his pomposity and his attention flew back to me.

"So you still have life for humour," he said. "So how about laughing at this. I was only joking. I have no intentions of hammering you—not after what Kat told me."

He waited a beat until I showed some recognition of what he meant. Could I trust anyone? Of course not. Kat had revealed my painful secret. Maybe she thought it would save me from the well, but I doubted it would save me from madness.

He must have seen the anger in my eyes, for then he said, "Oh, don't fret so, she's still on your side, you know. I had to… drag… that info out of her. She's round the back now, whimpering like a little bruised puppy. I will cheer her up later with the charms you denied Ozzy."

"Bastard," I spat.

He laughed and crouched beside me, sniffed and stood again. "I didn't think this through, did I. Still, I doubt a bit of mud will put off the lads. I could kick myself for not seeing the pointers earlier—when I tried to kiss you on the cheek, when Needle grabbed your breast, and Jim fondled your nether regions, your reactions were so extreme. I imagined it was because you are old and not used to such things any more, but it's more than that, isn't it, Molly? So much more." He crouched beside me again as I sniffled and looked around for hope. "Is there a name for it?" he asked. "This sexual aversion you have?"

"Trauma induced spontaneous combustion."

"Heh. What more could I expect from you. Now, I have explained the situation to these gentleman and they are very keen, despite your age, to study your reactions in a purely clinical trial."

153

"Please don't." I began to curl into a ball, protecting myself.

"Or you could tell me where… Finish the sentence."

"They're up your arse."

"You are remarkable. Even knowing what the lads are going to do, you don't lay up on the sass."

"And there fades the Molly we know and love," I said faintly, beginning to hide inside myself, withdrawing, letting myself become only a body without a mind.

I was scanning the floor. When it had happened, all those long years ago, I'd had no warning, no chance to look for a weapon beforehand. What was here that I could use? This time it was two lads, then it had been two lads. Their actions had scarred my life forever. What did I have now that the young Molly had not had? I had tried learning Tae-Kwon-Do since then, but was pretty useless at it, and at Uni I had used my wooden sandal to strike out—though I had been hit back with it and I had no shoes on now at all, so that was no good either.

And the answer came to me. An answer I didn't like because it would hurt me as much as it hurt them, because either I could let my fear weaken me or I could use it to empower me.

"I will leave you to your play, gentlemen," the major said, standing to leave. "I do not think I have the stomach to watch *this* kind of torture."

Jim grabbed me and I started kicking, while Needle ran his hands over me, pulling at my revolting clothing, his clammy hands stroking my skin and it was unbearable, like flames rippling across my body. Did I scream? It was more of a groan, panic and all the flashbacks, hot horrid images of *those* boys back then and now *these* boys, and in between the safety of a sexless almost loveless marriage which I had not wanted, yet it was easier than breaking down the barrier, for there was no counselling in my youth. You got on with stuff. So your attackers gave you an STI that likely rendered you infertile?

Deal with it. You buried the bad, or hurt others to cover your own feelings.

I had collapsed into myself as a teenager and never stepped out again. I can't even look at a man without thinking about that day, about what they did to me, remembering the hard hands and the male smells and young Molly's tears and the boys' laughter, and all the other tiny things that can ravage my dreams some nights. Now a simple kiss on a cheek is a bad enough trigger, so to have these lads' hands pressing into me, squeezing and prodding and trying to force my body this way and that, here was the horror that would hold me and freeze me until I had regressed far enough inside myself to not react at all.

If my plan didn't work.

"Stop!" I squealed, back arching as I forced my thighs to clamp together. "I'll tell you where the diamonds are."

"That didn't take much," Jim complained. "No fun at all." He adjusted his trousers and sat on his haunches, watching for me to change my mind.

"I don't want *him* to have them," I said in a low, conspiratorial voice. "Do you think he deserves them; that stuck up nitwit? Give me something to write on and I'll draw you a map; show you where I hid them, but please don't touch me again. Deal?"

They looked at each other, a greedy silent agreement passing between them. Jim took his inflexible, grasping hands off my arms as Needle rummaged in his massive pockets then shoved a small crumpled notebook at me.

I found myself tensing, fear in every pore, my breathing short and shallow as I fought my own body's reactions. The pain in my chest was real, the thrumming of my heart bad. Could I really do this?

"Pen?" I asked. "Pencil? I'm not going to write in blood, you know. Where's a writing implement? Are you telling me you carry a notebook but no pen? Hurry up."

I was screaming inside. It was taking all the energy and confidence I had built up over the years from arguments with Ozzy to keep my body still, to maintain the illusion of calmness because, once I moved on them, I would have to keep going, seeing it through to the harsh end of either them or me. I was about to find out if forty years of heavy gardening work had paid off in the strangest possible way.

"Here; this do?" Needle handed me a wax crayon, well chewed. My heart missed beats. This could ruin everything. I stared at the green crayon and moved it into position as I asked tentatively, "You got kids, Needle?"

"Nah, it's me nephew's."

"And, excuse the question, but have you ever killed anyone?"

"Not that it's any of your business, but yeah. Me and Jimmy here, we've done our bit for population control."

At his words, I could feel an anger rising in me that was greater than the fear.

"Good," I said, "because I'm about to kill *you*." And I lurched forwards to plunge the crayon deep into his eye. As he fell backwards wailing, I managed to push the shocked and slow reacting Jim backwards against the well wall where I grabbed his ankles, heaved, and unbalanced him into the well as easily as lifting a mega-bag of compost.

I turned back for the agonised gibbering Needle and cracked his head against the floor until he shut up, then dragged him to the well, yanked him up and tipped his skinny arse over the edge like a knobbly sack of potatoes. I heard a clunk. I hoped they'd knocked their stupid heads together

I thought I was going to faint. My heart was complaining again; racing, hopping, missing beats. I was breathless. I had to get out of the cellar and away quickly. How?

But I needn't have worried. That day, Fate had angled everything my way.

The door shocked me by opening quietly; so quietly I thought I was hallucinating, but I ducked behind the well to hide. Then Huggy's hushed voice said, "Ms T?" and I saw his wide shape in the dimly lit doorway. He held a jemmy in one hand and the other reached beckoningly towards me. We crept out of the house, into the dark and cold and peace of the night, far away from loud music and cold-blooded Majors and hot-blooded Katarinas and wells containing far more than water, and he practically carried me down the road to the waiting not-so-evil Micra.

Chapter 14

Hell's Boots

"ARE YOU SAFE, Hugo?" I asked as the Micra wound along the lanes connecting Highnam and Hartpury and I snuggled deeper into the fleece Huggy had thought to bring for me. I pressed him to reply. "Come on. It won't be good if he realises you helped me escape."

He shrugged. "I take my risks, Ms T. So does Kat. It was her turned off the alarms for five mins so I could get you out. 'Rescue poor old lady,' she said. He'd beaten her, poor kid. She needs to escape as much as anyone, but she won't risk it, so she reckoned the least she could do was help you." He gave a heavy sigh then went, "Sorry 'bout Misty, George had to hand her over when he asked. You know how it goes."

Yes. I did.

"Oh crap, I forgot." He pointed to the glove compartment; I opened it and found my glasses.

"You didn't happen to get my handbag too?"

"Nah, sorry, Kat didn't give me that. Had your lad's pic in it, right? Shame, but come on," he said, turning where I directed him into Over Old Road, "you go shelter with your mates. I don't think the Major'll bother chasing after you—"

"Not bother? Hugo, I think I killed Jim and Needle."

"What? How? Blimey!" he spluttered. "Still, couldn't happen to a more deserving couple of vermin. Nice one, Ms T."

"You needn't be so happy about it. If I killed them I'm down to the major's level. Not what

I wanted for my life." I pointed widely to Copsely Ridge and Huggy parked a little away from it.

"Major won't know where you are," he said reassuringly, "and I sure ain't gonna tell."

"That'll be a first. You've told him about other things, Hugo. And Kat told him something I had expected her to keep quiet. So… this time, please *do* keep quiet."

He chewed on his lip. "You know what it's like. Threats and punishments. It's not easy."

"Look, stay here for a while. You'll be safe with my friend. We'll find something for you, somehow."

He sighed, hands running loose around the wheel as though he were turning a corner. Was he considering my offer? I wanted to rescue him since I had failed to rescue Gavin.

"Nice you caring, and all, Ms T. Appreciate it. I'll think on it. Now, I gotta go get an alibi for the time, get your lads pic back to you. We can talk then."

⁓

My horror was over. All was well. I could risk breathing again.

163

And, because it was all over, I found the overwhelming urge to tell someone about the major, so I told the startled Callum, who had answered his door in his dressing gown at three in the morning to a stinking, dishevelled old lady, illuminated by the security light into a scrawny spectre.

After a warming shower, a change of clothes—his jeans, shirt and jumper fitted me well—and over a cup of tea or three with bread and marmite sandwiches, and a good dose of paracetamol for my bruised and aching head, I told him everything that had happened.

"Bloody hell! Forgive my French, Molly, but how long've you been stuck in that nightmare? And that hairy man at your house, your watcher, was he a danger to Dad that day he stayed? You should have slipped me a note or something."

"I think slipping you a note would have been far more dangerous for Joe than picking apples with Hugo. He wasn't even a threat to me. He doesn't want to be on the bad guys' team, I'm sure."

"Okay, so what's the next thing to do? Call the police. We can do that now."

"No! No police. Too dangerous. Let me lie low. Just let me stay awhile. I mean a few days until I sort out somewhere else to live. Somewhere a long way from Hartpury."

He was frowning. "But that major, he lives over in Highnam, you say? Can't you get the police onto *him*?"

"Callum, which bit of *dangerous* don't you get? Hugo said he'd seen the major kill someone with his swordstick."

I touched my bruised head. It didn't hurt so much anymore, but I would have a black eye, for sure.

"So he should be reported," Callum was saying earnestly. "With this Hugo as a witness we could get him out the way."

"No. Stop it!" My thoughts whirled in that dusty old bin called a brain.

Joe appeared at the top of the stairs.

"I want cocoa," he said.

165

I whirled on Callum, pointing to his father with a shaky finger. "*That's* what you should be focused on: Joe. He's improving in leaps and bounds, isn't he?"

"Yes, he's definitely showing shows of improvement."

Joe came down the stairs and waved at me, then went into the kitchen.

"Then focus on Joe," I said, "and ignore the problem I *had*, because it's over now, okay?"

He looked dubious. "You owe it to the villages to get that major out of circulation."

"No," I said, all determined to put the past behind me and forget it. "Let me go on as if life hadn't had a massive hiccup."

"You are really blasé about this, you know. Mad majors running around isn't going to do anyone any good."

"But it isn't going to be just him, is it? Report the major and someone else will step up to take his place, and they might get *you* if they know you're the one reporting him. Isn't this how it all works? By keeping people too scared to do anything? I had my cat murdered, so imagine if they threatened Joe."

There came a crash from the kitchen. "I dropped it," Joe said as he came back to the living room looking abashed.

Callum shook his head and got up. "Sorry, Dad." He went into the kitchen and, as I heard him sweeping up broken china, Joe patted me on the back.

"There, there," he said kindly. "It's all right, Milly. We all make mistakes."

"You are feeling better, aren't you?" I asked. He just smiled.

"So one thing puzzles me," Callum said, loitering in the kitchen doorway as the kettle hissed behind him, "Where *are* the money and the diamonds?"

"I've no idea, but I hope they're somewhere the major never finds them. Somewhere someone really hard up finds them by accident, and gets to have a nice life because of them."

The next day was spent struggling to sort both the car and the house insurance over Callum's phone. Enough to drive you mad when you've not got the details they want and me getting all flustered and forgetful. I also hoped the phone calls weren't enough to lead anyone to me that I didn't want to see.

But in the afternoon while Callum was out getting the medicines I'd managed to order on the phone, and Joe was peacefully watching YouTube, I went to the door as the bell rang, peered through the peephole, and saw it was the major.

"Molly?" he called. "Are you there?"

'Damn you, Huggy!' I thought, then yelled, "I'm calling the police."

"My dear Molly," came his silken voice. "Please don't phone the police just yet. Let me say my piece."

"Lord above, shut up with whatever you're playing at now and scarper."

"I came to give you some good news."

"So give it then leave me alone to call the cops."

"I don't think you will call them. You are as deep in this as I am. They investigate me, they investigate Molly Marshman, am I right?"

"Get lost." I walked away from the door. He hadn't mentioned the lads down the well. That, I presumed, had to mean they had survived.

"I have my property back," he called. "Most of it. Turned out the culprit was close to home after all. And you don't want me to get lost. I have your handbag here."

"Leave it on the doorstep then, you sicko!" I spluttered. "I don't ever want to see your face again. You froze me in that well, had me assaulted and you *killed my cat*!" The tears flooded out again. "And… and… I will probably be traumatised for years to come, just because you wouldn't believe the word of a lady."

"Listen, Molly, quell the fires of your indignation. Maybe you can help me. It was Huggy."

"Huggy who told you I was here? Yes, I'd figured that out."

"He took the money bag."

My vision blurred for a moment. Oh, of course it was him! Who was it saw the opportunity to take the money and blame it on the old lady passing by? That was why he'd been so moody around me.

"And I would never kill a cat."

"What? What are you playing at?"

"I let her go. Outside my house. Just ran off free as a bird. Haven't seen her since, but then I haven't seen my diamonds at all. I was wondering if Huggy might have given them to you, for safe-keeping, out of some misplaced sense of friendship. You see, he couldn't tell me where they are."

"*Couldn't?*"

"I was a bit over zealous, shall we say. I didn't have Needle to advise me, for some reason."

I felt dizzy as the import of his words sank in.

"He was quite a bad guy, our Huggy, but he liked you," I heard the major say through the door and my ears rang with a strange dizziness. "He told Needle not to touch you, dared to stand up to me."

"All in the past tense," I murmured to myself, leaning on the door as tears came and my heart trembled, reminding me I hadn't taken my meds in days. Maybe the major would be the death of me after all. I felt my heart was breaking.

"You have to understand," the major's irritating voice went on calmly from the other side of the door, and if I'd been capable of it I would have opened the door and hit him with the table. "Since I still don't know where the diamonds are, there's still a problem

"Well, at least you can't take my house to pieces again," I erupted. "You and your bloody diamonds can rot in hell 'cause I have no bloody idea where they are, you utter fecking idiot-monster!"

"Actually, if you think about it, *you* killed Huggy," came his muffled voice, still annoyingly calm. "If he hadn't gone back to get *your* handbag, and if *you* hadn't incapacitated Needle who understands the drug administration far better than I, I believe he might still be alive."

171

I heard the click of his cane as he walked away, heard the distant sound of the car starting up and leaving, then I sat on the settee while I tried to calm my wildly palpitating heart. He had managed to blame Huggy's demise on me, the bastard. But, oh no... why was I still so sympathetic and missing the man who had caused the whole wretched mess? I had liked Huggy. I had hoped for him. I felt I could have taken him in and looked after him like a surrogate son. Set him on the right path—

I stopped. He was gone, just like Gavin, and that was that.

So I made myself a cup of tea, drowned it in brandy, and comforted myself by planning how to look for Misty. I'd ring the RSPCA and report her missing, and call both villages' Post Offices to put up adverts. After all, there was a river between Highnam and Hartpury. I couldn't expect her to get back on her own.

I found myself, for a funny mind-slipping moment, wondering if Huggy would help by driving up and down the local roads looking for her, and then my tired brain stuttered back into gear and reminded me he wasn't just lost, he was gone forever, so I sat and dripped tears into my tea as I cried for them both.

Chapter 15

Deathwatch Beetle

J WAS WATCHING the local news that evening when it was announced.

...body of a man identified as Hugo Jenkins, a known Cheltenham felon... believed killed in a gangland hit, was discovered in a Hartpury field by... The newscaster said it with a grim and sincere face.

The picture... no...!

The image burned into me. I could hardly focus through a deluge of tears.

With the yellow ditch-digging JCB showing half in the background, a pair of Wellingtons were shown sticking feet first out of the mud. The striking O.W. on the boots told me who it was.

"Oh, Hugo!" I wailed.

Callum was sat at his desk on his laptop, but he looked over at the cry that flew out of me, saw the image on the screen, jumped up and turned off the TV and sat beside me on the settee.

"Callum, that was the lad who helped me. How could the major do that to him? Bury him like that? Thank god he was dead before they did it."

I was shaking to my core. Had the boots been left exposed as a hideous message to me?

But that would mean I was still a suspect. I supposed if the diamonds still hadn't been found, I had to be, but worse still was the idea that if I'd let Callum go to the police when he'd suggested it, perhaps Huggy's murder could have been prevented.

Callum's mobile rang. He jumped to it, listened to the voice on the other end and just said, "Yeah, sure, no problem," but I didn't care what it was about. I was in my own uncomfortable, mentally damning myself world. Maybe Callum would end up looking after both Joe and me, both invalids of life.

Joe was sat at the dining table watching his personal DVD player, jiggling and making small noise of excitement like a teenage boy. Oblivious to the world around him, for a second I envied his state.

Callum sat beside me again. "Poor sod," he said, and I assumed he meant Huggy. "Didn't he give you any idea where he'd hidden the diamonds then? We need to get that major out of your life."

"Oh come on, Callum. I really don't want to talk about this now."

"Okay, okay," he said in a calming voice. "I'm around if you do need to talk. But didn't he give you any clues? If he had the cash it follows he had the diamonds. And it sounds like the kind of thing you could do with right now, now the house is burned down and you need to get back on your feet and so on."

"Clues? No. We caught newts and a chicken and talked about edible plants and the merits of owning cats and played on mobile phone games, that was all we did, not discuss where to hide diamonds. If he did have them—and I agree I suppose he did—the answer's gone with him and, like I said before, I hope someone who really needs them finds them."

While Callum returned to his laptop, the grandfather clock tick-tock, tick-tocked and I was warm and comfortable and all was peaceful in that tiny world. Callum had picked up my heart meds from the doctor earlier, plus a hefty packet of antibiotics to take because of the well water, and all would soon be fine inside me. And all would be okay outside me too, I told myself.

Eventually I said, "I need the loo now. All that crying triggers it.

"Tears are natural," Callum said. "Cry all you want, Molly. Losing Huggy and Misty, I can understand the grief."

As I went up the stairs to the toilet I heard him on his mobile again. 'I really must get one,' I thought. 'One that actually works, not like the one Huggy gave me.'

And then I was sad all over again.

I stopped at the landing window on the way back, and drew the curtain aside. I gazed at the stars, bright and lighting up the sky alongside the almost full moon. I wondered if Misty could navigate home by stars, or the moon. I had no idea.

Then something struck me.

Huggy.

I had never told Callum his nick name, just called him Hugo, I was sure I had. But minutes ago, downstairs, he had distinctly called him Huggy. The last thing I wanted was to suspect Callum too, but the more I pondered on what had been said, or what I had not chosen to say, the more confused I became.

Then the answer to my wondering come in the most undesired way.

Car headlights swung into the drive. I opened the window and craned my neck to see round the corner, but I didn't have to see. After the clunk of a door shutting, I could hear the *click, click, click* approaching like a deathwatch beetle.

I heard the front door shut and his hideous voice wafted up the stairs.

Callum had let the major into the house, and known Huggy's name, and asked about the diamonds in a rather persistent way.

Ergo, Callum was also a BBG.

I wanted to run, to hide, but within the house there was nowhere to do either, but boosted by the healing chemicals now coursing once again through my veins, I stepped down the stairs like a duchess, head up, eyes ablaze and said, "Hello, Major Nitwit. Fancy seeing *you* here."

"Aha, Ms Molly. Fancy seeing you here." He beamed.

"I've nothing for you, you know that."

"Oh, but my dear, I'm just visiting my friend Callum. Callum, my boy, didn't you tell her?"

I stopped on the middle stair. "What now?" I said in disgust and weariness. "Are you his brother-in-law or something? A transgender long lost aunt? No, I don't care, nothing would surprise me, just go, Richard. Don't be a dick, although I suppose you can't help it with that name."

The major laughed. "Got quite a tongue on her when she gets going, hasn't she."

I stood still and looked across at Callum miserably. Finding out he was also one of the BBGs seemed par for the course my life had taken that month. And Joe? He couldn't be bluffing, could he? Would he jump out from his chair any second and all three men would join in with laughing at me?

"I don't care what you mindless manipulative morons are up to now," I said, "but I'm going to go for a walk to get the stench of you out of my nostrils."

"Hmm, quite a nice bit of alliteration there," the major said.

As he turned to Callum an idea leapt into my head. Risky, but maybe...

"So, Callum," he said. "You're convinced she doesn't know where the diamonds are?"

"I would say it's a safe bet she doesn't, sir," Callum said, fixing my agonised eye.

"Well then, time to tie up the ends, wouldn't you say?" He drew his sword from the cane smoothly.

'Well practised,' I thought in dread, and took a step backwards, upwards, trying to stay calm before I executed my escape plan.

"Sir, is that really necessary?" Callum said, shooting me worried glances. "She's only an old lady."

"She's not just an old lady, she's a mouthy old lady who would have no trouble telling the police everything she had seen and heard now it's all over and she feels safe, am I right, Molly? She's also Oswald's old lady and I wouldn't mind betting she knows a fair few things about our business, eh?" He smirked at me, voice suave and calm and even. "Shame you weren't at that meeting when I poisoned Oswald. Could have been rid of the two of

181

you. Saved all this fuss and mess. Anyway, don't pretend to care, Callum. It wasn't that long ago you were begging me to get rid of your old man, and a useless job Myrna did of that; made him even more of a burden."

"I promise not to say anything," I said, pleading, the idea that the major had somehow poisoned Ozzy not surprising me at all.

I stepped back again.

"Wait!" Callum said, facing the major head on. "You *told* Myrna to push Dad?"

"You wanted Joe 'off your back'." The major said, his voice no longer calm, rising angry as Callum challenged him. "Your words exactly, man. You wanted to move up the ladder and his criticism of our lifestyle was holding you back. You don't get too many choices, you stu—"

"No, Myrna!" came the great cry as Joe launched himself at the major. "No no no!" Joe yelled and he flattened the major as Callum yelled for him to stop, but as they tussled I turned tail and fled to Joe's room, clambered out of the window onto the low roof beyond. I looked at the drop. I had climbed a tree and got stuck, but this was life or death, so I dropped inelegantly onto the plants below as screams and crashes rang from out of the open window behind me, and I fled a new horror.

Chapter 16

Dark Woods

*J*OE HAD SAVED me with his obsession over Myrna, or Myrna had saved me by hurting Joe to the point where Joe was obsessed with defending people.

My head span as I limped up the road, ankle complaining where I had landed badly, and soon I was staggering. I heard a door slam behind me and assumed he was coming for me, so I put on another spurt but I wasn't going to last long.

I stopped and looked back, hands on knees, panting, and there he was in the moonlight, coat flapping like evil wings as he ran towards me.

Damn that there were so few houses and cars on that road, but if I alerted anyone, they would be in danger too.

I ran into the woods as soon as I reached them. Stopping to get my breath back, surrounded by the sweet innocent scents of trees and bushes, I felt the woods to be mine. My friendly trees; my haunts. I knew all the twists and turns of these woods, even in the pale moonlight. The bushes reached their branches to me as if to comfort, and I padded on, hearing him follow me, hearing the crashes and cracks as he tracked me. As I stopped, so did he.

I don't know how people in movies can move so quietly. It is virtually impossible. Also, I had no doubt that his strides were longer than mine, and likely didn't have heart problems, but I would push on until the game was won.

I took him around in a circle. A calculated circle. I hoped he was wondering just how big the woods actually were and feeling lost, though he had a torch. I could see its feeble beam as I crouched to one side in a thicket and let him pass by.

He was far enough away again so I pressed on, trying to keep to the clusters of scrambling brambles and red-hipped dog roses where my skin and clothing were caught and scratched, but it meant the same would happen to him and hold him up. And annoy him. It was worth it just for that.

When I came to the main path bisecting the woods, I hopped-ran downhill and then nipped back into the darkness. I found a sturdy stick, one that would not break under strain, and waited behind a tree trunk for the pompous dick and clobbered him on the back as he passed. He went sprawling, the torch flying out of his hands, but still lit, so that plan to remove the torch hadn't worked.

"Molly," he roared into our silent arena. "Come out and fight fair."

I think he hoped my snarky nature would make me answer, but I didn't, busy considering another plan to deprive him of torchlight.

Or maybe it didn't matter.

Finally reaching what I had been heading for, I used the sturdy stick to lever off the heavy metal cap. I was lucky it hadn't been concreted on. I couldn't look down. I had no idea how deep it was or if it even held water anymore, but I was pretty sure the hole would be too much for him to climb out of easily, if at all. With the major out of the way for even a short while, I could risk going back to Callum's to call the police.

I hastily gathered some smaller sticks and pushed them across the gap, black and scary in its emptiness. Every five seconds I had stopped and listened, beginning to think he'd given up, then hearing his footsteps a little closer each time.

I stood and panted quietly, listening, waiting for my moment to drop the major down the well.

"Hello there, Mollykins," he said, scary as a spectre in the woods, the failing light of his torch making him a dim figure across from me. I stepped backwards, he stepped forwards. I looked left to right as if planning a new route to escape and he laughed. I sank to a crouching position with a fake sob-sigh of weariness and he lifted the sword.

"End days, I think," he said. "The elders will understand when I say you were going to tell the police everything Ozzy had told you."

"Sure," I said. "Mysterious elders understand about things like that."

"You can become a mystery yourself," he said. "The Hartpury horror. Children will tell the tale of how you haunt these trees, and spook themselves for generations to come. How is that for a legacy?"

"You know the divide between us. I don't half-drown kitties or scare children."

"Now, now, don't lie. Jim and Needle are about a third of your age, Molly, and look what you did to them. Threw them down my well. And now I have two men in hospital, Jim with a cracked head and Needle minus an eye. Get it? One eyed Needle?" He chuckled a ghastly sound. "That crayon move was clever. I didn't know you were so resourceful, but that's what makes you so dangerous."

I waited for him to move, the stick behind my back in case I needed to hit him again. I could see in my mind's eye him falling straight down that hole, screaming and then begging me to get him up, asking me to forgive him, making empty promises and still yelling as I walked away to call the police on his miserable hide.

I will admit I felt a visceral pleasure in that wait. But when he did step onto the brittle sticks and lurched forwards, his body half down the hole and half up, he dropped the sword and his hands grabbed for my ankles, trying to drag me down with him, and I screamed with pain and fear, my howls filling the woods and sending pheasants clattering with fright.

I had to reach one hand into the nearby flesh-ripping brambles to save myself, while with the other hand I beat at him with the stick. I hit him again and again, bashing him until he relinquished his grip and slipped and fell, and I heard the deep splash.

"Molly!" his plaintive echoing cry came. "Mol-lyyy!"

I walked away, nursing my bramble-savaged hand, limping up the path and back to Copse-ley Ridge for the phone, full of a perverse pride. Not pride that I had dumped another man down a well, but pride that I had bested another of my demons. I felt neither guilt nor grief nor shame, only a vast relief that I would be freeing many, many, people from his evil influence.

Then I reached Copsely Ridge and had to scream again. Both Callum and Joe were in the front room, almost where I had left them, but underneath all the blood that covered them it was hard to tell who had been who.

Chapter 17

Haunted Hartpury

I don't know what became of the major's body. The police had come to me at the local hotel I had booked into, and told me he'd been dead by the time they'd found the well. I was questioned relentlessly over the next few days, but never charged with anything.

Katarina gave herself up to the police. If I'd still had a house I might have been tempted to have taken her on as a housekeeper, because she

191

did me a great favour. She had been looking after Misty, who she had rescued from the major's garden and kept hidden in the big house.

Callum and Joe were cremated in Gloucester and I was the only non-press person who went to the service. I had hoped the mysterious Myrna would put in a show, but she didn't. She hadn't been a silent partner, though. Since she was still married to Callum, she had sorted the funerals and put Copsley Ridge on the market before you could say Jackanory.

I claimed Hugo's body as no one else had come forward, so he's interred in the village graveyard, and I got him a nice headstone because I could never have one for Gavin.

Finding out that Ozzy was a BBG was liberating. I no longer felt bad about hating him. Gavin fell into the river after a drunken fight with mates; that's what we'd been told. Now I think it likely that Gavin, a strong swimmer, was not drunk as they'd claimed, but hopped up on drugs, which made sense now I know what his father had been.

And I had not seen any of it, living my life blinkered by his adamant 'women stay at home and don't have technology' attitude.

Since the fire, I had reaffirmed my relationships with many people in the village. To be honest, I suspected the many invites for a chat in Hartpury were mainly to get me to talk about my story, but I felt the place was less hostile to me, more giving, and I liked that. The imagined hostility was my fault, I could see that now. Locked in my own perceived miseries, I had driven people away. Hartpury is a beautiful little village filled with welcoming people and I was looking forward to many more years there once the house had been rebuilt. Life was almost sorting itself out again, like waves breaking down the castles built in the sand, smoothing everything out.

However, the story wasn't over yet.

One chilly day in late October, I had walked to the churchyard, and I was stood looking at a new headstone erected a few days before at my cost. It read, 'Hugo Jenkins, taken too soon, stone dedicated by Molly'.

He deserved more than he had been given by life.

Someone approached me. I heard the damp tread of footsteps in the overgrown grass, so I turned and there he was: a tall, middle aged man, wearing a raincoat and a stern face.

"Mrs Marshman?" he asked abruptly.

'This is it,' I thought with an odd kind of acceptance. He was a hit man, sent to kill me. So I drew myself up tall and acted as if I didn't care. No one was going to say I hadn't met my end with courage.

"Yes." I managed to smile. "Though I haven't gone by that name in a while. Can I help you?" I met his eye and kept on smiling.

As he put a hand inside the coat, I think I did squeak in fright because he put out the other hand in a placatory way and said, "It's alright, ma'am," and he withdrew a warrant card and flashed it at me, though whether it was real or not was anyone's guess. "D.I . Courtland," he said. "C.I.D."

I swallowed hard. "Nice to meet you."

"There's a car out front of the church. I'd be grateful if you'd accompany me to it."

"I'm sorry," I said. "I don't think I trust anyone after what I went though. I don't want to go in a car with you. Where do you want to take me, anyway? The police station; a big deep hole?"

He pulled what could have been an amused face. "Castle Carron churchyard."

"That doesn't... er...cheer me at all. Sounds like you want to bury me outside of Hartpury."

Now he smiled. "I can appreciate your hesitation, Mrs Marshman. I am familiar with the situation you've survived. Now I am following *police* orders to take you to Castle Carron, maybe a half hour run. Back before tea, I imagine."

"And why are you taking me to this place I've never heard of? What's there for me?"

His smile evaporated as he said, "Your son."

Chapter 18

Death Fails

I SAT IN THE back of the not so comfortable unmarked police car as it sped down
the motorway. It certainly looked official on the
inside, with a police radio and lots of other in-
struments on the dashboard, so I tried to relax.

I was full of a nameless sad-joy. They were
taking me to Gavin's final resting place, on the
coast just past Bristol, where I suppose his body
had washed up. That raised the question of how

they'd known it was Gavin. Then I realised it must have been Ozzy's machinations at work again. He had known but kept the location of the grave from me. The final denial of ever having raised a child who had defied him. The final insult to me, for refusing to even try to make a 'real' son for him.

I drew a great sigh. 'All right, deal with what you have now, Molly. No point in forever thinking about yesterday. Today will be the start of a new chapter.'

The car drew up outside the gateway of a picturesque little church in a tiny quaint village, and the trees and bushes around the graveyard were all a glory of gold and red, shining with the dampness of recent rain and shaking in a strong breeze.

I walked behind D.I. Courtland as he entered the churchyard and we came up to the first row of upright stones, then he nodded to me by way of farewell and went back to the car.

I pulled up my coat collar to keep off the wind and looked around. Which one was it? There were so few I could look at them one by one. The row at the back looked newest, so I walked that way, but none of the headstones said anything like I would have expected. Puzzled, I looked up and around. The police car still sat by the gate, and there by the church wall the big D.I. stood in his raincoat.

But it wasn't him; this other man was bearded.

'Huggy?' I said to myself, puzzled.

I walked quickly towards him but the man walked off and, as the wind rocked the trees around me, I rounded the corner of the but-tressed wall and saw him enter the main door of the church.

The door was slowly closing as I got there, so I pushed it open again and stepped inside. Damp and musty carpet and old book smells hit my nose. I shivered a little.

Where was the man? I looked over the short rows of polished pews and saw no one. For a jar-ring moment I thought I had followed a ghost.

I walked a little down the aisle then turned and looked back, and there he was, in the corner by

the font, the play of wind-dancing lights coming through the stained glass windows playing
tricks on me.

"Quit playing around, Huggy," I said, ecstatic
to see him alive. "I'm *so* relieved to see you again.
Come here and give me a hug, why don't you?"

The man stepped into the light.

He wasn't Huggy.

"Oh, come on," he said in a voice I had never
got out of my head. "A few years and a beard and
you forget all about me?"

I stepped towards him, arms out. "If the seas
froze over and the world caught fire, I could
never forget you, Gavin."

❧

It turned out that Gavin had heard all about
my escapades on TV. Four deaths in a little village was big news.

We sat in the church and talked a while. He
hadn't run away those long years ago. He hadn't
fallen into the river, no, not at all. He'd been in
his despicable father's drug group and decided to

go undercover for the police when Ozzy kicked him out for taking those same drugs. Although he hadn't managed to take down Ozzy's group, he had provided valuable information that had taken much off the market and convicted a lot of people. My son; the spy. And when he'd done enough he was taken into the witness protection scheme, and left his old life and me behind.

So when he said he wanted to see me, it was safer for me to be taken to the church than for him to come see me.

Misty and I moved out of Hartpury to live with Gavin and his family on the coast, in a house a stone's throw from the sea, just like I've always wanted. The blonde girl Huggy had seen in the pub is Gavin's wife, a charming creature, and their three children are amazing! Instant grand-motherhood!

Gavin hunted down for Lottie for me. She passed some years ago leaving two sons, but although I can rest happy in the knowledge I have some relatives left I cannot, of course, ever meet them. They wouldn't know me from Adam anyway, and I doubt I'd feel anything for them, I just needed to know.

So here we are, a separate little flat for me, the freedom of their garden to potter in, a pond with goldfish, a gardener to do all the heavy stuff, and children to play with. Heaven, for both me and Misty, who has settled in well.

I landed on my feet and, although terror had gripped me for a lot of my life, I was healing from the inside out. I could hug again. Hug my grandchildren, my daughter-in-law, my son, and not feel like I wanted to scream at the contact. That was progress. Old dogs (not me, because I am not old) can learn new tricks.

I had felt like a piece of rubbish cast aside to moulder socially throughout my life because of one horrible incident. Beating Jim and Needle and the major taught me I could fight back and, believe me, the new Molly will fight back for the rest of her life. I had discovered that even in the meekest heart there is a power to call on. It may not be a nice power, but its name is survival, and that comes down to the fittest mentally as much as physically.I'm off the radar. Mrs Marshman became Ms Turner, became Ms Smith. I don't pay tax, don't draw my pension even, have no involvement with the social services or show up anywhere—after all, I don't know who's left that might want to still play hunt-the-diamonds.

Which I have.

You heard right. I have the diamonds, ghastly little uncut things that look like nothing really, like crazed beach glass. I can't believe people died for them.

Gavin's growing family absorbs money, so I gave them to him, because I wouldn't know the first thing about how to sell them and he does.

The major had slipped up and overdosed Hugo before he could spill the beans, and because Major Nitwit had been so keen to make a point to me and left the initialled boots on him, and because I chose to see to Hugo's funeral myself—receiving the boots in his effects—the system efficiently handed back what the BBGs had searched so long and hard for.

I won't say I *knew* they were there, but I did suspect. Seeing Hugo with the tools in the shed, and the fact I'd noticed he'd worn the boots all the time, favouring them over his Doc Martens, made me examine them very carefully.

He'd borrowed tools to carve out the inside of the boot heels, creating compartments.

Poor Hugo; I still feel sad for him, but I like to imagine that my big, bearded friend Huggy would be happy to know it was I who found the stones.

⌐

My grandchildren listen to my latest attempt at a poem with big eyes, while all I can think is, 'Last laugh's on you, Major Nitwit, not me, not the woman whose friend you killed, not the woman you dropped in a well so vile she had to have a fortnight's worth of antibiotics, not the woman you pursued murderously through the woods… No, it's you who the children will mock forever… *You* are the Hartpury horror.'

~

"In Hartpury woods, there is a bane
a crazy man with a greying mane
who brandishes a fearful cane
and scares the children who call his name.
Major!
Major Nitwit! they cry,
Pursued by the devil, his spirit to blacken
he's in through the bushes, and out through the
bracken
though scratched by the brambles, his pace
does not slacken
'til tripped in the well to die."

THE END

About The Author

J.D. Warner is a poet and writer, who has spent her life reading and writing quirky stories in fantasy and sci-fi worlds. A lifelong geology nerd, she also keeps Amazon parrots, who sometimes bite to remind her she lives in the real world.

In 2000, her sci-fi epic serial Another Side of the Sky ran for a year in Keep It Coming Magazine, and in 2019 she released the fantasy novel Hex-Tych, to good reviews. Her short stories appear in various publications and she was once a winner in the short story contest held at The Cheltenham Literary Festival.

.

Lightning Source UK Ltd.
Milton Keynes UK
UKHW010916190321
380627UK00003B/181